FRAYED

JEAN DAVIS

Also by Jean Davis

The Last God
A Broken Race
Destiny Pills and Space Wizards
Dreams of Stars and Lies
Spindelkin
Everyone Dies
Not Another Bard's Tale

The Narvan
Trust
The Minor Years
Chain of Gray
Bound In Blue
Seeker
Tears of the Tyrant

For Gale
This one is all your fault and neither of us even remembers exactly how.

1

Sam clutched two envelopes in his hand as he crossed from the yellowed tangle of his yard to the vibrant green of the neighbor's lawn. With his mother's instructions still ringing in his ears, he headed for their paved walk lined with purple petunias to avoid trampling the perfectly shorn turf.

Pots spilling over with pink and white blooms and tall, spiky greenery sat on each porch step. Henry's new red bike stood under the safety of the covered porch with its slow-moving ceiling fan and hanging ferns. The little two-wheeler had replaced the shiny red tricycle Henry had ridden for the past year and a half. Sam eyed the rusted ten-speed propped against his own garage. It had never been new, not in his eighteen years anyway. With their garage full of boxes from his grandma's estate and the old car his father had never gotten around to restoring before he'd run off, there wasn't room to keep his bike out of the weather.

He took a deep breath and pushed the doorbell. A cheery chime rang on the other side of the big picture window next to the front door. The curtain tugged aside for a moment before the door opened.

"Good afternoon, Samuel. What brings you by?" asked Mrs. Harris as she wiped her hands on her frilly apron. A finger print of flour marred her perfectly made-up face, like a model out of one of his sister's magazines.

"The new mailman must still be learning the route," he said, holding out the two envelopes. "Momma asked me to run these over."

Mrs. Harris took the envelopes, glancing at them momentarily before sliding them into a pocket in her apron. She locked him in a once-over—the kind that all mothers did, like they went to some sort of training when they took a baby home from the hospital.

"You tell your mother she can come over anytime. She doesn't need to be putting up with that man yelling at all hours. There's help, shelters, the police. You hear me, Sam?"

"Yes, Ma'am."

Momma said to always be polite to Mrs. Harris. Or else. He didn't want to get on the wrong side of Momma's 'or else' even though he hated when people brought up Nick. He was supposed to be polite to Nick too, but it was easier to avoid him when he was around than to try and fake it.

Mrs. Harris smiled. "You're a good kid, Samuel. Don't let anyone tell you otherwise. A true gem, considering." She cast a disparaging glance toward his house. "Now, if you'll excuse me, I've got cookies in the oven."

He nodded, shuffling his yellowed sneakers a step backward.

"Thank you for bringing the mail," she said.

A rosy-cheeked face pressed against the window. "Is that Sam? Can he play?"

"Not today, Henry. You've got piano lessons in half an hour."

"Tomorrow?" he asked, now at the door.

Not that hanging out with the five-year-old was high on Sam's list of things to do, but if it involved sampling a couple of home-made cookies, that beat trying to wade through his algebra homework.

"You've got soccer tomorrow, honey." Mrs. Harris reached for the door.

Sam couldn't decide if her stance was to keep Henry inside or to make her own escape. "I should go." He took another step backward.

Out of the corner of his eye, he caught a blinding flash of light, like semi-truck headlights in the dead of night. The more he tried to look at it, to try and figure out what was inside the house, right over Henry's shoulder, the more scrambled his brain became.

"Are you alright?" Mrs. Harris asked from a distance. "Samuel?"

He blinked. The light vanished. Henry was gone from the door and Mrs. Harris watched him with both hands on the doorknob, one foot already inside.

She probably thought he was on drugs or something. Momma always did. So did half his teachers, for that matter.

"Just dizzy there for a second," he mumbled before making his escape.

As he traversed the sidewalk toward the road and back to his own yard, Sam closed his eyes. The image burned into his eyelids clearly showed what he'd been unable to look at. The negative shape of a man stood behind Henry. It wasn't the shape of the man, but the fact that he had wings that sent Sam running for the door, into his house, and straight into his room where he slammed the door shut.

"Sam? What happened now?" Momma's footsteps pounded toward his door. "Did you get into a fight again?"

Again? Twice. Two times. Ever. And neither of them were his fault, but she leapt to that conclusion damn near every time he came home upset.

If anyone excelled at fighting, it was her and

Nick. He wasn't at all surprised Mrs. Harris had even heard them.

"No, Momma. I'm fine. Just have lots of homework today," he said tightly from the safety of his room. 'I saw an angel today' wanted to leap out of his mouth, but she'd just jump to the second usual conclusion: He must be on drugs.

At least he was pretty sure that was what he'd seen. What else looked like a man but had wings and glowed? Sitting in his room, surrounded by his things, he began to wonder if he'd seen anything at all. What kind of person sees angels at the neighbor's house? Why would one be there anyway? It wasn't like little Henry was in danger in his perfect house, surrounded by an actual home security system. He knew it was more than just the stickers some people put in their windows to fool robbers because a guy in a company van came by now and then to talk to Mrs. Harris. Not that he was watching the Harris house that closely, but since his father left they hadn't had cable TV and there were only so many times he could play through the two games he had for his nine-year-old PlayStation.

Momma's shadow lingered under his door. "Do you work tonight? Maybe you could bring dinner home?" she asked.

The last thing he wanted to eat again was four-hour-old burgers and stale fries from whatever order had been made wrong during his shift. Mr. Sanderson, his boss, always made sure to set the returned stuff aside for him. Not that his boss had ever asked if he needed the food. Maybe he just looked like he did.

"I gave you money for groceries three days ago."

He kept thirty dollars out of each paycheck, just enough for lunch money at school for him and Sianna. Everything else, he handed over to pay for groceries and utilities. It wasn't a lot, but it filled some of the gaps in their government assistance.

"I know, baby. It's just that it's our anniversary this week, me and Nick I mean, and I wanted to get something nice to wear. One of those fancy department store dresses, you know? Not something from Goodwill."

Nick had stormed off last night after calling her some nasty things and she was still assuming they would celebrate an anniversary? "Do you think he'll be back?"

"Of course he will." Momma waved off his comment like it was silly.

It was that she wanted him to come back that he had a hard time believing. For now, he'd enjoy every minute Nick was gone and the house was quiet.

"I don't work tonight, but I'll figure something out with what we've got," he offered.

"Thank you, Sam. Love you." Momma flitted away.

He sat on his bed listening to the muted beat of the music from Sianna's room down the hall for a long while with his algebra book still in his backpack on the floor. When he did finally pull the book out, it sat heavily on his lap. It wasn't like he was going to college next year. As it was, he'd be lucky to pull together enough credits to graduate. Though he tried hard, taking care of Momma and Sianna took a lot of his time and energy. And then there was picking up as many shifts as he could so he could help pay the bills.

Sam sighed. College might not be in his future, but he did need to graduate unless he wanted to flip burgers for the rest of his life. He opened his book and located the work page from the folder in his backpack. He'd just found a pencil when a bright light outside his window caught his attention. Had Henry left a favorite toy outside and now his mom was out looking for it with a flashlight?

But the light didn't move. Sam pulled back his curtain to peer at the Harris house. A beam of light shown from Henry's room upstairs down on the lawn below. The light filled Sam's whole window, too large to be a flashlight. More like a search beacon, and it was barely dusk.

Sam squinted at Henry's window, wondering what the kid was playing with that was so bright. It had to eat up a lot of batteries for sure. That had to be what he'd seen earlier, some expensive toy. Just because Henry didn't have a dad either, didn't put them in the same boat. Mr. Harris had died in a car crash four years ago. A semi-truck driver had fallen asleep. Momma said Mrs. Harris was set for life on account of the company paying out a boatload to avoid a lawsuit and their auto and life insurance. Not that Sam wanted his own father dead, but since he had vanished without a word, there didn't seem to be much difference. His family sure could have used the financial assistance any of those could have offered.

Guilt hit Sam hard. He knew he shouldn't even think those sorts of things. Surely Pastor Joe would say it was a sin. Probably one of the big ones. Not that he'd been to church since his father had left. Momma didn't like the way people looked at her there anymore. While he'd always enjoyed the free cookies after the service, and sometimes they'd gotten treats for memorizing bible verses during Sunday school, he hadn't liked how people had talked about his family either, all hushed whispers and not-so-sly looks.

He had homework to do. Sam let go of the curtain and did his best to ignore the bright light outside so he could focus on his algebra.

He'd just finished the first side of the page when the light grew brighter, flooding in around the edges of his curtain. Tugging the fabric aside, he found himself face to face with a tall, glowing man. With wings. Giant white feathered wings that arced from his shoulders to take up all the space between the two lilac bushes that marked the property line between the two houses.

A holy flipping angel stood right outside his window.

2

am gulped and jumped off the bed. The text book landed on the pitted wood floor with a heavy thump. Though his curtain was again closed, and there was a window and a wall between him and outside, it didn't seem to matter one bit to the angel. It just walked right through everything and stood there in the middle of his room, one wing still hanging outside and the other through the wall into the bathroom he shared with Sianna.

"Do you think you can ignore me?" asked a booming voice sure to be heard by Momma, Sianna, and every neighbor for several houses around.

"No?" Sam stammered, reaching back to the wall to steady himself. There didn't seem to be enough space in his nine by ten room for the both of them.

Where was Pastor Joe now? He'd know what was going on, what to say, how not to make the angel angry. It definitely sounded angry.

He tried to remember everything he'd learned about angels in Sunday school. Wings? Check. Halo? Not exactly, but the glow sort of made up for that. Harp? This angel didn't appear to be the singing type, more the avenging sort. Had God heard him thinking about the benefits of having his father be dead? But if he'd seen the angel at the Harris house, and his gut told him that he had, it was after him for something else.

"Is this about the three dollars in change I borrowed from the tip jar at work last week? I was going to pay it back."

The angel stared at him with soul-exposing force.

"The time I tripped Alan Jennings in the hall after I heard him call Sianna a slut? She's not, and neither is Momma, and I'm sick of people saying otherwise."

The angel took a step forward, its arm reaching out. Sam stood frozen, watching as if from a distance, wishing with all his might that he was little again and able to curl up into a ball in the back of his closet where he could become invisible to bellowing voices and giant hands.

The angel's hand seemed to envelop his entire head, fingers wrapping around him, tearing through his hair. The glowing face, or where the face should be, instilled a terror so great that he quaked all the way down to his toes. Pressure built in his eyes as the angel's burning palm pressed harder. Sam tried to give voice to the scream boiling up from his lungs but the angel held his mouth shut.

The world went still and silent as if everything outside his room had disappeared. The angel's hand retracted. It studied him with an intent face Sam realized he could now see. He could see everything as if a filter had been removed from his eyes.

The angel still glowed but with a soft light like a candle. Its wings had vanished behind its broad shoulders. Piercing blue eyes drilled into him.

"You see me now." Its voice no longer sounded like it was blasting through a loud speaker, but it now held an odd quality, like an echo that trailed every word individually.

Sam, his tongue tied in knots, nodded. How did one address an angel? Even seeing it now, wearing loose white pants and a long white shirt, there was nothing distinctively masculine or feminine about it. Beautiful, to be sure, but with an intensity that still burned if he looked too close. Was this what people should have looked like, what God had intended before everyone started breeding hilly nilly once sin had taken hold?

"I am Aralim."

"Sam," he managed to say.

"You're to be given a task."

"Me?" he squeaked.

The more he looked at Aralim the more confused he got. Its skin and features shifted from Beth Parker whitebread to Sani Abubakar midnight and everything between as if it refused to be defined by any one ethnicity. Its hair stayed the same shoulder length but also shifted in texture and color. Only its blue eyes did not change.

When he shifted his gaze from Aralim to take in his room, its image stopped shifting. The angel wasn't the only thing that looked different now. Every scratch on his hand-me-down headboard stood out in glaring detail, each dent in the floor, the bare threads of his seven-year-old thrift store comforter. The pages of the fallen-open algebra book looked sharp enough to cut flesh. He held up his hand to see every pore and hair as if staring through a magnifying glass.

"You can see now," said Aralim.

Sam nodded. "Everything looks so..."

"Like it was meant to be seen. This is what was taken from the first sinners."

Talk of sin made Sam's skin crawl. "Why me? What did I do?"

"Nothing yet. I'm here to tell you what you will do."

"And give me a chance to fix it?" He could try harder. If it took going to church every Sunday, he would ignore the looks and whispers. Gaining the notice of an angel couldn't be good. He must be about to do something terrible.

"Fix? No. You have an assignment."

Sam wished Aralim smiled, or had any expression at all beyond stern and soul-piercing. His stomach twisted. "I don't understand."

"Sometimes people are born but events change after the fact, requiring that soul to be elsewhere at a different time."

Sam's legs shook with the effort of facing the angel. The weight of the unknown task pressed down on him. He desperately wanted to sit but the angel was standing. It would be rude to do otherwise. He didn't have any chairs in his room and his bed creaked under his weight alone each night.

"So they were born by mistake?" he ventured.

"God doesn't make mistakes," Aralim declared with a thunderous force that verged on bursting Sam's eardrums. "Events change. Man changes things. Freewill." The angel grimaced.

While Sam had wanted a different expression from the angel, this one didn't settle his nerves in the least. "So, how does a person's soul get where it's needed when events change?"

"They have to die."

"But can't God just make that happen? I mean, he is—"

"That would imply that God made a mistake.

He doesn't."

"So...how does—" he hesitated finding a conclusion, not wanting to try Aralim's patience any further.

"Man changed events. Man must maintain the order of souls."

Though Sam considered that he should probably be praying to someone else, he found himself praying that Momma would burst in any second and Aralim would vanish. Then he could pretend this whole angel thing never happened. He would have even welcomed Sianna violating their bedroom privacy agreement if it would mean Aralim would maybe disappear.

But no one came to save him.

"What am I supposed to do?" he asked.

"A soul must be freed from its body. That is your assignment."

"I get to pick the soul?"

If he had to free someone, maybe he could find a person who was elderly or sick. Someone who deserved to leave the world would be even better, but he wasn't exactly equipped for that. He avoided trouble, fights, weapons, and anything that might get him fired or kicked out of school.

Aralim shook his head. "Every soul is special, specific to the overall path of man. There is a plan, a picture man can't see."

Could he see it now with his new angel vision?

Sam was about to ask when Aralim announced, "Henry Harris is needed elsewhere."

3

Sam disregarded all manners and plopped down on the bed before he fainted. "Little Henry? The kid next door?"

Aralim just stared at him.

"I'm supposed to kill Henry?"

"No, you were not *supposed* to. But that's what is now required of you to correct the actions of others, to maintain the weave of Man's tapestry."

Sam shook his head, the idea of such a thing refusing to sink in. "I don't think I can. I know I can't."

"You will," Aralim stated firmly. "You have one year to complete this task. The longer you wait, the worse it will be for everyone."

If he had a year, he could find help to get out of this assignment from God. Or was it from God?

Maybe the solution was to talk himself out of Aralim's favor. If he was in favor at all. It was impossible to tell.

Sam summoned all the bravado he could find. "Does God know you're here trying to fix his non-mistake?"

"He knows everything," the booming voice blasted into him, making every cell in Sam's body shake.

"If I do this, I'll be arrested. My family will lose the house. Sianna might have to drop out of school. We don't have money for a good lawyer. Not that a lawyer would help if I'm guilty. I don't suppose..."

Aralim continued with the dead-pan stare.

"No legal assistance then." Sam drew his quivering body up into as defiant of a stare as he could manage. "Then I must decline. My family needs me. Besides, Henry's just a little kid. He's never even said a mean word to me. I couldn't hurt him. I won't."

Aralim snapped his fingers. A scroll appeared in his hands—an honest-to-goodness real scroll on thick paper with fancy script writing.

"What is that?" he asked, not really wanting to know.

"Your contract."

"I said, I'm not doing it."

"You will." Aralim unfurled the scroll and set it on the bed beside Sam.

"What about free will?"

"Doesn't apply to you. You've been conscripted."

"That's a thing? I seriously don't get a choice? You're just going to decide my life right here and now? I get no say?"

"It's already been decided. You're the best choice, Samuel."

"I don't agree."

Aralim's stern demeanor cracked. A sad smile broke through. "You can't see the full picture. Trust me, you are the best choice."

Sam spared a glance at the scroll. The writing reminded him of the Declaration of Independence he'd seen in his history book. "Do I get anything out of this?" he asked quietly.

"You will be rewarded when your soul comes back into the weave."

"Will I remember? I mean, will I know if this thing you're asking of me is worth it?" He hated himself for even considering such a thing. Could anything be worth killing Henry? Every fiber of his being said no.

Aralim pointed to one of the long paragraphs in the middle of the scroll. "You'll come back as your sister's child."

"Sianna is only sixteen. You'll still be with your family, just differently."

Aralim just stared.

"But will I know?"

The angel's gaze broke away. "No. That's not how it works."

Sam focused on the words on the scroll. With each line he read, he noticed the words around it shifted languages. Too much of the text focused on legalese, on words he didn't know, on concepts he couldn't grasp. Frustration burst up from his quaking belly and out of his mouth.

"I don't know what any of this means."

The angel snapped its fingers again. A quill pen, the fancy kind like people had at weddings, appeared in the angel's hand. "It doesn't matter. You're going to sign. You're going to kill Henry Harris. In return, you'll get another chance at life."

What Aralim wasn't saying made Sam stop cold. "Do you mean that not everyone gets a chance at another life?"

"That is correct."

Sam took the quill, wondering if he could write with such a thing. Or where he was supposed to sign. Or if he could, given what Aralim expected of him.

"If there aren't any lawyers involved, why have the contract?"

"Think of it as paperwork attached to your soul. We like to be thorough. With so many souls to keep track of, special arrangements would be easy to overlook otherwise."

The unspoken threats to his eternal soul began to fully sink in. "So I'd be doing God a favor?"

"Hardly. God finds these sorts of situations

very frustrating. You'd be doing Man a favor."

"Man won't see it that way," Sam muttered, pressing the quill to the paper experimentally.

Aralim glanced to the left. Sam tried to see what it was looking at, but there was nothing there. The angel's mouth moved like it was talking but no sound came out. The quill grew awkward and heavy in his hand. The tip hovered over the line at the bottom with his name printed underneath in the fancy script.

"We need to wrap this up," Aralim said curtly. "I'm needed elsewhere."

"I don't suppose I could bargain for a lottery win for Momma? Something to help her and Sianna out?"

Aralim scowled. "You will be helping them. We don't negotiate."

So his fate was decided. The future of his own soul hung in the balance. Pastor Joe hadn't ever mentioned that God made strong-arm threats. God was supposed to be all 'love thy neighbor', not *kill* him.

But one couldn't argue with God.

Sam signed the contract.

4

The angel vanished as soon as Sam pulled the tip of the quill away from his signature. The quill and contract were also gone, leaving no trace that anything out of the ordinary had happened.

"Sam, I'm hungry. Momma said you were going to make dinner," Sianna said from outside his door.

"I'll be right there."

Sam took one last look around his room, not daring to pull back the curtain to see the neighbor's house or possibly catch a glimpse of the little boy he was supposed to kill. He laughed nervously. None of that could be real, could it? He'd imagined it all.

Sam rushed to his door and opened it. Sianna stood there, startled. He could see every pore on her face and strand of hair framing it, the weave of her shirt, and flecks of gold in her brown eyes.

"What were you doing in there? You're like... glowing." Her face scrunched up. "Oh gross. Nevermind."

He flushed. "Not that. Come on, you can help figure out what we're going to make for dinner."

"Only if you promise to wash your hands first."

"I said, *that* wasn't what I was doing."

Sianna laughed, knocking her hip into him. "Whatever. You're still going to wash your hands if we're going to put together a patented S & S special."

It wasn't until mid-dinner as Sianna was telling how some girl he didn't know got whacked in the face with a soccer ball in gym class that Sam realized his hyper-detailed angel vision had faded away. Momma laughed along with Sianna, the familiar sounds of their voices warmed him through and through. This was his life, just another day, nothing crazy had happened. He'd made it all up, some freaky dream he'd slipped into to get out of doing his homework.

He shoved the last bite of the heavily processed round slice of white maybe-meat rolled around a slathering of canned cranberry sauce into his mouth. They had to get creative with the bi-weekly box Pastor Joe delivered. It wasn't half bad, considering how some of their S & S specials went. Sianna passed him a bowl containing the last scoop of the buttery mashed potato pouch she'd made. They were only a dollar at the grocery store. He had a feeling that he knew nearly every dollar item the store carried. That was Momma's favorite price.

"You go ahead," he offered, knowing she was just as hungry as he was.

"You're too skinny for a boy your age," his mother scolded. "You need some muscle on you like Nick."

He didn't need to be anything like Nick, but she wouldn't be deterred. She took the bowl from Sianna and shoveled the velvety potato glop onto his plate.

"I'm gonna go out back and have a smoke with Alberdeen. You two finish your homework, do the dishes, and clean up in here." Momma put her plate on the counter beside the sink then grabbed her purse and headed for the back door.

"You can always tell when she and Nick are fighting," Sianna remarked. "She goes through a pack a day, I swear."

Another of Momma's expensive habits they couldn't afford. Maybe he'd be better off buying the groceries himself rather than giving her money to spend on cigarettes and anniversary dresses for a man she fought with more often than they got along.

"They were loud last night. The fight, I mean," he said, clearing the rest of the table.

Sianna rolled her eyes. "Yeah, that too. I wish I could go back to being too little to know what all the noise was about. The not yelling kind," she said with a grimace. "It's gross. She's our Mother. I don't want to hear that."

Sam nodded. Momma did everything loudly. She was probably out on the upstairs back porch boisterously gossiping or complaining about Nick to her friend right now.

He was glad Alberdeen had moved into the upstairs of their house four years ago. While that meant he'd lost his large room, he did get the room that had belonged to Sianna on the first floor that wasn't so hot in the summer. Sianna had moved into the bigger room that had belonged to his parents when they were together. Momma had moved into a makeshift bedroom in the basement for what she called 'privacy' but there weren't any doors down there and not enough insulation between the floors to make anything private. However, having Alberdeen rent the upstairs was the reason the bank no longer called every week about late or missing payments.

Now the woman and her two cats lived in the place that had been his. She took baths in the deep claw foot tub he'd loved when he was little, like it was his own swimming pool. Back when he'd played outside on a green lawn, pancake Saturdays were normal, and he'd sat out in the garage in the evenings learning tools while his father tinkered with his car. Back then, he'd had a future, at least, a very different one.

"Earth to Sam?"

He shook his head and realized Sianna was trying to hand him a dish towel.

"Your turn to dry."

"Right. Sorry."

"You're being weird tonight." She shut off the water in the sink. Bubbles fizzled around the dishes.

"It's been a weird day."

"Not weird enough. I need an asteroid to hit school so I don't have to take a history test tomorrow."

Sam laughed. "I wouldn't mind the school getting wiped out."

They worked their way through the pots and plates.

"I could help you study if you want. In case the asteroid doesn't show up?"

"Sure, yeah." Sianna finished washing the last of the dishes and let the water out.

The house phone rang. She ran to answer it. "It's Paolo, do you mind?"

So much for studying. She'd been spending an awful lot of time with Paolo lately. One plus of not having their own cellphones was that he knew when she was talking to him. It was when she was on a date, out of contact that had him worried.

Paolo was a Junior and not one of Sam's favorite people. Why couldn't Sianna like one of the quiet guys? Maybe someone from the marching band. But no, this was the third guy she'd dated from the soccer team, and he didn't like what popular opinion had to say about that.

"Sure, but don't talk forever."

Sianna stuck her tongue out at him before returning to her hushed conversation. To give her some space, Sam left the rest of the dishes in the rack to dry, hung up the towel, and started back toward his room. Except he didn't want to go back in there and question his sanity again. Since Momma was out back with Alberdeen, he went out to sit on the front step instead.

They didn't have a big front porch like the Harris house. Theirs was only a covered entry way with two posts on either side of the two cement steps. A chipped pot sat in the corner, half full of dirt. There hadn't been flowers in it since he'd gifted it to Momma for Mother's day a few years ago.

The cement was cold now that the sun had gone down. Sam shivered, wishing he'd grabbed his hoodie. In the weak moonlight, he could pretend the paint wasn't chipping off the formerly white posts and the grime on the siding was simply the grey color it was supposed to be.

Supposed to be. Sam rubbed his hands over

his face. He was supposed to be finishing his homework and maybe watching something on one of the three stations that came in without cable. Instead, he was sitting in the cold, his gaze locked on the house across the street with the spiral-cut shrubs, on anything across the street, anything except the house next door.

The light flipped on in Henry's room. Drawing Sam's attention no matter how hard he tried to ignore it.

He hurried inside and shut the door. Sianna was still on the phone. Momma was nowhere to be seen. Nick hadn't come back, which Sam wasn't at all sad about. He went to his room, took the blanket off his bed, and draped it over the curtain rod, further blocking out any light from next door.

He sat on his bed and picked up his book and the rest of his homework. He'd nearly finished his algebra when the pencil in his hand suddenly felt too much like the quill the angel had given him. Sam threw the pencil across the room, shoved everything into his backpack, and undressed. He slid into bed and pulled the covers close.

"Screw this day. Tomorrow will be better. It has to be."

5

Sam managed to avoid Mrs. Harris and her son for nine days. He went to school, did his homework, worked his shifts, listened patiently to Momma ranting when she and Nick didn't, in fact, make up before their anniversary date, and attempted to keep an eye on Sianna who was publicly hanging on Paolo far more than Sam liked. It was all going great until he got home from school and found Momma waiting for him in the kitchen. She held out an envelope.

Not again. "Make Sianna deliver it."

"She's out with that nice boy. Paolo, I think?"

"Yeah, you gotta have a talk with her. You know I'm not one to snitch, but they made quite a scene in the hallway today. Don't be surprised if you get a call from school."

She snorted. "I did. They called me at work. I was in the middle of doing Miss Pearl's hair. You know I hate interruptions at work."

Miss Pearl probably never noticed and kept right on chatting whether Momma was there or not. Most of the people at the nursing home where Momma worked were just happy for anyone to talk to but not all that aware of anything else.

"So, what did she say?" he asked.

"That my daughter was violating the public display of affection school policy." She shook her head and tossed the misdelivered envelope onto the counter. "When did schools start sticking their noses in people's personal business? Ridiculous. And to bother me at work with that nonsense."

"I meant Sianna. What did she say?"

"She thought the school should mind its own business too. I can't believe they give out detentions for kissing a boy."

He couldn't believe how badly she was missing the point. Wasn't she supposed to be the parent here? He hated getting Sianna in trouble, but maybe the school hadn't fully explained what everyone else had seen.

"They were doing some serious kissing. He had his hand up her shirt for heaven's sake. That certainly didn't help what people already say about her."

Momma gave him a stern look and jammed her hands onto her hips. "What have I told you about listening to gossip? I raised you better than that. Sianna is a good girl. She's your sister. You better hope I don't catch wind that you're passing talk like that around."

When had he ever gossiped? Hypocrite, he wanted to yell in her face, but then he felt bad for thinking bad of her. "Of course I don't talk bad about her. It's just that—"

"Not another word. You take that mail over to Mrs. Harris and then make sure your sister gets something to eat when she gets home. Nick is coming by in an hour to take me out for that anniversary dinner we missed last week. Speaking of which, I gotta get ready." She left the kitchen with a loud huff.

He stared after her. So Nick was still in the picture? He wanted to point out that it wasn't exactly an anniversary dinner if they'd broken up in between the dates, but whatever. At least Nick wasn't staying here again. Yet.

Sam swiped the envelope off the counter. He wanted to crunch it up and toss it in the trash, but the long string of names in the return address caught his eye. A lawyer's office. It was probably something important. With a disgusted growl, he stomped out the front door and over to the Harris' house.

The sight of Henry sitting on the porch swing with his mother made every muscle in his body tighten. Sam glanced around the house, dreading the sight of that one thing he'd decided he'd imagined and vowed never to speak of again. Nothing out of the ordinary appeared. He sighed with relief.

Mrs. Harris sat with one arm around Henry while talking on her cell phone. She glanced up at him as he approached. He smiled apologetically, held up the envelope, and reached out to set it on the top porch step so he could make his escape without interrupting her.

Mrs. Harris looked straight at him and held up her finger.

Could he pretend he hadn't seen it? Maybe he could play stupid and leave.

Henry hopped off the swing and ran over to the steps. He sniffed and wiped a tear from his cheek as he took the envelope from Sam.

Why did he have to be crying? Sam's resolve to turn and leave crumbled. "What's wrong?" he asked quietly.

Henry sniffed again. "My Nana is sick. Bad sick, and she gots no mommy to take care of her."

"I see. Maybe a doctor can take care of her instead?"

"Maybe," Henry said hesitantly.

Mrs. Harris stood, still watching him. "Yes, I understand. I'll figure something out. Thank you." She ended her call and slipped the phone into her pocket. "Hello, Sam."

"Hi, Mrs. Harris. Just the mail again." He

nodded to the envelope in Henry's hands.

She looked at it and frowned. "That can't be good news."

He shrugged, not knowing what to say. Her eye makeup had smeared. Henry hadn't been the only one crying. He didn't have time for this. He was just supposed to drop off the mail, then he had to get home and write an essay in the hour and a half he had before going to work.

"I gotta go," he said, trying to figure out how to make his exit less awkward given that they were both upset about something that was none of his business.

"Before you do, I was wondering if you could help me out," said Mrs. Harris. "My mother is ill and her care team just informed me that she's being sent home as per her wishes, but she needs full-time care. At home." She pinched the bridge of her nose and drew a deep breath. "Would you or your sister be able to watch Henry for a few hours three days a week? After school, of course. I can get home care in for most of the shifts, but I'd like to take some of them myself. Henry is in kindergarten three days a week, so I need someone to get him off the bus and stay with him until the evening shift nurse can get in on those days."

"I have a job after school." Sianna was too busy pawing Paolo to want to take on a babysitting job.

"I can pay you." She pursed her lips. "How

about twenty dollars an hour? Would that make up for missing a few shifts a week?"

That was twice what he made. Maybe he could save up for a low-end cell phone so Sianna could finally have one like she'd been asking for forever.

"What days? I can check with my manager tonight to see if I can switch my schedule around."

The relief on Mrs. Harris's face was so raw that he felt all warm inside.

"That would be great. I really appreciate it." She checked her phone and gave him the dates she needed to cover.

With the mail delivered and before he forgot the dates, Sam hurried home. He wrote down the babysitting schedule, cranked out his essay, and was about to put on his work uniform when the doorbell rang. It rang again.

Sam groaned. Momma should be ready by now, why wasn't she answering so he didn't have to?

"Sam, can you get the door?" Momma called up from the basement.

Gritting his teeth, Sam headed for the front door and opened it.

Nick stood on the front step with a limp be-dead-by-tomorrow rose in hand. His beaming smile vanished when he saw Sam. "Where's your mother?"

"She'll be up in a minute. Might as well come

in and wait."

Nick looked at his watch, a giant gold monster that had to be a total knock-off because he couldn't afford something real like that even if it was from the pawnshop downtown. "We're gonna be late," he grumbled loudly. "Come on, Shonda. We gotta go."

He ran a hand through his slicked-back hair, and then seeming to realize that he'd messed up whatever he had going on in his otherwise unruly mop, pressed the hair back down and wiped his hand on his pants leg. It left a greasy sheen behind on the grey slacks. The purple silk shirt and grey tie had to be new, judging by the factory-pressed creases and unstained appearance.

Momma hurried up the stairs, face all made up with too much makeup and carrying a pair of black high heel shoes in her hand. She wore a tight red dress that showed off more of her top half than Sam was comfortable with. It didn't cover much of her bottom half either. She would have grounded Sianna for going out like that.

She bent over to slip on her shoes. Nick's eyes went wide and he grinned. Having seen far too much, Sam escaped to his bedroom to get ready for work.

As he pulled his work shirt over his head, the light in his room flared. With his heart suddenly in his throat, Sam spun around to see Aralim standing in his room. Thankfully, the angel's wings were tucked away. Sam could only imagine how high Nick would shriek if he happened to use the bathroom as an angel wing shot through the wall.

"You've done nothing," Aralim stated flatly.

"I don't plan on doing anything."

"You signed the contract."

"You didn't give me a choice. I'm going to be late. I have to go to work."

"You have a far more important job to do."

"Then how about *you* do it?" Sam walked out the door and slammed it behind him.

Aralim walked right through it and followed him into the living room, where they were thankfully alone. "The longer you wait, the worse it will be for everyone."

"It won't be good for me either way, so excuse me if I'm in no hurry."

Aralim was suddenly in front of him. The angel grabbed Sam's arm. Its touch was hot, not burning, but uncomfortable and hard.

"You should hurry. Don't think about yourself, but your family."

"Are you calling me selfish?"

Did this angel not know him at all? Had God not seen everything Sam had done all his life? He'd had his selfish moments, sure, but who didn't? And how could anyone in their right mind not understand that he wouldn't want to be racing to meet his end or cause the death of another?

"I don't have time for this." Sam tried to shake off Aralim's hand, but the angel held on tightly.

Blue angel eyes drilled into his brain. Everything in the living room seemed skewed like he was standing somewhere else, or at a different height, or maybe both.

He saw Momma at the kitchen table, her head in her hands. Sianna, looking gaunt and tired, rubbed Momma's shoulder. "It will be okay. We'll figure something out," Sianna said.

A chill settled over Sam and his sister uttering the same words that Mrs. Harris had a couple of hours before.

"I don't want to leave you. And the house," Momma said. Tears splashed onto the table in front of her.

"Don't worry about the house. The bank can have it. I can get a room at the women's shelter on 5th. My caseworker already has a standing request in." Sianna's voice sounded calm, but her face, behind Momma where she couldn't be seen, was anything but.

"You shouldn't have to do that. You shouldn't have to lose everyone. I'm so sorry. I should have gone to the clinic sooner. If they had caught it earlier..." Momma's far-too-thin body shook as she sobbed.

The room slipped back into focus, but Sam

found he was flat on his back staring at the ceiling. Aralim stood beside him, his arms crossed over his white-clothed chest.

Feeling dizzy, Sam scrambled to his feet. "What was that?"

"A possible future. One I think you'd like to avoid."

Was it him going to jail and legal expenses that had ruined his family or something else? Was Momma going to get sick? Was that what was sending fracturing his family even more than his absence? When Aralim had said that things would get bad the longer he waited, he hadn't taken the time to consider what that might mean. No matter what he did or how fast he went about it, Sam had a feeling nothing good would come of it for his family.

If he was supposed to come back as Sianna's child, he'd have to wait five to ten years in jail before he died of something. Would he get stabbed like prisoners did in TV shows? Would it hurt? Was it too much to ask to peacefully die in his sleep?

"Sam!" Aralim shook him by the shoulders.

Not looking forward to any of it, Sam sighed. "I told Mrs. Harris that I'd watch Henry a few days a week. If I'm over there, maybe the opportunity to do what you've asked of me will present itself, alright?"

Aralim nodded, looking only slightly appeased.

"You're going to be late."

"No thanks to you."

The angel reached out and tapped Sam's forehead with a finger. In the blink of an eye, Sam found himself in the alley behind work with his bike already locked up in the rack. He didn't remember getting on his bike or even walking outside his house to get it.

Damned angel. Sam stood there a moment, trying to calm himself. All he kept seeing was his mother crying and the scared, lost look in Sianna's eyes.

With a shuddering breath, Sam opened the back door and went to work.

6

Sam sat in Henry's room, holding up the Squidman figure while Henry ran in circles around him, making Piranhaman fly. The kid squealed as he tripped over the train they'd played with earlier. Sam reached out and caught Henry before he could face plant on the plastic tracks and jumble of building blocks.

"You have to be careful. You almost crashed Piranhaman."

Safe on the floor beside Sam, Henry laughed. "He's got scales and big teeth. He'd be okay."

"You're not. Your mom would be mad if she came home to find you covered in bandaids." Sam tried to keep his tone light but all he could think about was what Aralim wanted him to do and what Mrs. Harris was going to do when she found Henry far beyond the help of a first aid kit. And now he was sitting here playing with the kid. Laughing with him. Why couldn't Aralim pick a different soul to be needed? Someone else far from here. Someone Sam didn't know.

"I'll be careful," Henry said, jumping back to his feet and more cautiously flying Piranhaman while making chomping noises.

Maybe if he had a year to complete this task, something would happen to make him hate Henry. Or maybe hate Mrs. Harris. He tried to think of something bad enough that would make killing Henry not feel so bad. Not one thing came to mind.

Maybe he just needed to give Henry or Mrs. Harris enough time to come up with something on their own.

Henry's stomach growled loudly, sending the kid into a fit of giggles. He chomped his teeth at Sam. "I'm hungrier than Piranahman!"

Sam couldn't help but laugh. "Well then, since your mom won't be back until bedtime, I suppose we should eat."

Mrs. Harris had given him free rein of her kitchen. Unlimited food. That was almost better than the pay.

He glanced at the clock on Henry's dresser. She was due for a check-in soon anyway. The phone was in the kitchen.

"Come on. Bring Squidman. He can help cook."

Henry guffawed. "He's got a butler for that."

"We don't. Come on." Sam got to his feet and

shooed Henry out of the bedroom and toward the stairs.

Henry held the rail in one hand and his toy in the other as he walked down carefully. "We used to. Sort of. A cleaning lady butler. Daddy hired her since he was gone for work a lot. Mom says he always did nice things like that. Was your Daddy nice too?"

"I don't remember, but I can tell you we never had a cleaning lady," Sam said tightly.

Henry plopped down on the stool beside the island in the kitchen. He stood Squidman on the counter in front of him.

It wasn't Henry's fault he'd had it better. Sam sighed inwardly. Was dying in an accident better than deserting your family? He supposed the end result was the same. Their dads were both gone.

Sam glanced around the kitchen, deciding where to start. "My dad did most of the cooking and kept the house nice. But now he's gone too."

Henry nodded. "You're the dad now? That's what my Momma said, that I got to be the man of the house since my Daddy is gone."

Sam had never thought of it like that. "I suppose so."

"So you could keep your house nice? Momma said someone needs to or things will start to fall apart. She said she would feel bad having to call the city and maybe getting your family in trouble."

"Is that what she said?" Why couldn't Mrs. Harris mind her own business? This was what he needed to hear, stuff that would make him angry.

Henry was busy playing with Squidman and didn't answer.

From the kitchen, Sam had a clear view out of the big bow window on the side of the living room. His house stood there in plain sight for all to see. For Mrs. Harris to see. In the comfort of her own home, all done up nice and clean.

All the houses on the street had the same look, some had covered porches and some only covered front steps, but they were all two-story, some variation of grey, tan, or white, had the same peak roof, the same general floor plan. They'd all been built within a couple of years of each other. Yet, his house appeared to be a good twenty years older than the rest. The landscaping was overgrown, seedlings grew in the gutter, and the gutter on the side of the garage hung half off thanks to a big branch a few years back. The lightbulbs on the outdoor lights had long given up. Momma's rusted-out Camry sat in the driveway that grass was slowly overtaking.

Maybe if she didn't like what she was looking at, Mrs. Harris could put her flipping fancy fabric-covered blinds down. Sam realized he was gripping the edge of the countertop with as much force as Aralim had used on his arm the last time he'd visited.

Henry looked at him and scrunched up his face. "Are you okay?"

If he snapped at Henry now, he might not get to come back. As much as he wanted the money, it was the incentive to complete his task that he desperately needed. Mrs. Harris's disparaging remarks about his house were a start, but hardly enough to make him want to kill anyone.

"I'm fine." He forced a smile. "What do you want to eat?"

Henry shrugged. "Babysitters usually make me hotdogs, sliced up so I don't choke."

"I don't usually babysit so how about we try something different." Sam opened the refrigerator and whistled. Every shelf was full. Fruit and vegetables filled two drawers and each had their own as if they'd been carefully sorted. An assortment of condiments filled an entire shelf and one had three kinds of soda, all stacked in little cans, the fancy ones, not the regular size. He never understood why anyone would pay more for a smaller can but apparently Mrs. Harris did.

"You want a soda while I figure out what to make?"

"No," Henry said quickly. "I'm only allowed to have milk, apple juice, or water. Soda is for moms only."

Good grief, they had both white milk and

chocolate milk, and as he looked up one shelf, a container of strawberry syrup to make strawberry milk. Who did that, have three flipping kinds of milk in their fridge at once?

"What kind?" he asked, shaking his head.

"White. The strawberry kind makes my stomach hurt and chocolate isn't good with food."

Well, wasn't he just the one to know about it all? Sam opened a few cupboard doors until he found the glasses.

He poured one half-full of white milk. Henry regarded it with wide eyes. "A real glass? I don't think I'm allowed to have one of those."

"I won't tell, just be careful."

Henry grinned and took a big sip. Milk left a mustache on his upper lip when he carefully set the glass down.

Sam left him to his Squidman and milk and wandered over to see what might be in the freezer. He pulled the bottom drawer open. Jackpot!

Without any further exploring, he slipped over to the spotless oven. Did Mrs. Harris ever use it? It looked brand new. He didn't remember the one in his house ever looking this clean. None of the appliances actually, even though they had to be about the same age. He pre-heated the oven and hunted down a couple of cookie sheets.

"We're going to feast tonight, little man." Sam grinned merrily as he shook out pizza rolls, tater tots, fries, fried shrimp, jalapeño poppers, chicken nuggets, and fried mushrooms onto the trays. Once the oven beeped, he slid them in and took a stool beside Henry to wait for the first round of the timer to go off.

For a moment, he felt guilty, wondering what Sianna was going to eat. Maybe he'd bring a plate home for her. Momma was out with Nick. At least he hadn't moved back into the house again. Yet.

When the food was done, he filled two plates and then pulled out an assortment of condiments from the top shelf. He almost needed another plate for all the dipping sauces. Sam ate with a single-minded focus, enjoying one of the best meals he'd had in a long time.

Henry broke his concentration. "My stomach hurts."

"Sounds like you've had enough then."

Henry eyed his plate doubtfully. "But I'm supposed to finish everything on my plate."

"You don't have to eat all that." Sam picked up Henry's plate and pushed the leftovers onto his own. "There, all clean."

Henry grinned. "You're the best babysitter."

Hardly, but Sam smiled back, all the same.

"May I be excused?"

"Of course."

Henry let out a loud whoop and jumped off the stool with Squidman in hand. "It's cartoon time. I get one hour. Start the timer."

Sam was about to ask if he was serious, but given everything else he'd learned about the kid, he probably was. He hit the timer on the microwave and sat back down to gorge himself at a more leisurely pace now that Henry was occupied in the living room.

When he couldn't force another bite down, he searched for a plastic container and poured the last remnants inside. The matching cover was easy to find in the wide, organized drawer. He slipped the container into his backpack to bring home for Sianna or to snack on later if she'd already eaten. Then he cleaned up the dishes and washed off the counters. Assured everything was back to its spotless state, he settled into a chair at the kitchen table. In view of the couch in the living room, he got busy with his homework. Getting paid to do homework, he laughed to himself.

Mrs. Harris arrived home promptly at eight. She walked through the door looking weary. Though her comments about his house had made him angry, he couldn't find it in himself to take any of that out on her now, not with her looking exhausted, his stomach full of her food, and leftovers hidden in his backpack.

Mrs. Harris set her purse on the table in the entry way.

The entry way in his house was a landing

zone for shoes and a wobbly chair that was piled with coats. This one looked much nicer, everything tidy and not a speck of dust on anything.

"Everything go okay?" he asked just as she asked the same thing of him.

He laughed. She smiled weakly.

"Everything was fine here." He glanced at the timer. "Little man has seventeen minutes of screen time left. He ate everything, but his room is probably still a mess. Sorry, we didn't get back up there to clean up."

"That's fine. Thank you, Sam." She held out four twenty-dollar bills. "I appreciate you being here with him. He likes you."

Sam took the cash, marveling at the crisp bills in his hand. It almost felt wrong taking it, at least taking so much of it. He'd gotten a great meal for free, did most of his homework, and hadn't minded sitting on the clean floor of Sam's room playing for a couple of hours. He'd never had even a quarter of that many toys when he was a kid.

"We had fun." He looked at the money again and handed two of the bills back. "He was no trouble at all, and I kind of ate a lot of the food in your freezer."

Mrs. Harris smiled again, but this time it reached her eyes and her face lit up. "You keep it. See you again on Thursday?"

He nodded, pushed the cash into his pocket,

and shouldered his backpack. "I'll be here to get him off the bus."

Sam said goodbye to Henry and then headed for the door. It wasn't until he was halfway home that he realized Mrs. Harris hadn't answered his question. He'd have to ask her how her mother was doing again when he saw her on Thursday. And return the plastic container he'd borrowed. He walked through the front door to find Momma wrapped around Nick on the couch. She hopped up and straightened her clothes.

"I thought you were in your room. Were you at work?"

"No. Watching Henry Harris."

"The rich kid next door? Doesn't he have a nanny or something?" asked Nick, who made no effort to get up from the couch but looked vastly annoyed that Momma had.

"No, he doesn't. I have homework to finish. Is Sianna home?"

"She's on a date with Paolo."

Again? Given how she'd been acting with that boy, he might only have to wait a few years in jail for her to get pregnant. But Sam didn't want to think of his sister that way. She wasn't what the gossips at school said about her. She wasn't.

"How about we go downstairs?" Momma suggested to Nick.

Sam groaned under his breath. That meant

Nick was going to stay over. And once he was back here for a night, he'd be back for good. Or at least until they had another fight. He didn't like either of those two options.

Henry's words came back to him. Was he the man of the house now? Should he say something? Was it his place? Momma paid most of the bills. And she was his mother. He shook his head and headed for his room.

Glad that Aralim wasn't there waiting for him, Sam finished his homework, tucked his newfound wealth into the pages of one of the three books on his shelf, and then went to bed.

The moans from the basement made him cram his pillow over his head. Then he thought of Sianna and how he hadn't heard her come home. And how Momma hadn't even noticed Sianna missing her curfew on a school night. Once Nick was on her mind, everything else seemed to vanish.

7

Mrs. Harris set Sam's payment on the table beside his backpack. "Would you like to come to church with us on Sunday?"

"It's been a while."

"God doesn't care how long it's been, just that you're there," she said with a smile.

Why did she have to be nice? He'd been hoping Henry would reveal something beyond his mother's opinions on their shoddy house, but he hadn't. The kid was fun and Mrs. Harris paid him well. She didn't even mind how much he ate whenever he watched Henry. In fact, she seemed happy about it, like she knew how much he needed good meals, and it wasn't even in a condescending sort of way.

"I suppose I could. I'm not on until the dinner shift on Sunday." And with Sianna spending all her time with Paolo and Nick living at their house again, he had no urge to be home. Momma didn't notice if he was there or not.

"Great, we'll see you on Sunday morning."

Was going to church asking for angel trouble? The hairs on Sam's neck tickled, causing him to shiver. It had been two weeks since he'd seen Aralim. Maybe the angel had found some other way to solve God's non-mistake. Sam could only hope because the more time he spent at the Harris house, the more against fulfilling his task he became.

He walked out the front door and could hear Nick yelling before he'd hit the sidewalk. Did Momma have all the windows open or were their walls that thin?

There was a loud crash and a woman shrieked. Sam bolted for the door. He stepped into the entryway and dashed into the living room to see Momma's prized heirloom vase shattered in the middle of the floor. Momma stood there wailing while Nick ranted. The only words he picked up on were "No good whore" before the raging pulse in his ears drowned out everything else.

With no regard for Nick's considerable height and muscle mass, Sam marched right over and planted himself in front of the grown man. "Get out. Now."

"Samuel!" said Momma, aghast.

Sam spun around to face her. Tears streaked down her cheeks.

"Would you rather it's you on the floor? I'm

sick of this. He stays out. You want to see him, that's up to you, but don't bring him here."

"You can't tell me—" spurted Nick.

Momma gave Sam a long look but then nodded just a little. "It's time for you to leave. We're through."

Nick looked ready to burst, his fists clenched at his sides.

Sam's heart pounded and his nerves sang. He didn't start fights, but he was ready if it came to that. He wasn't about to let Nick hit his mother and he sure looked ready to do just that.

"Shonda, if I walk out that door, no amount of begging will win me back."

"No one wants to *win* you." Sam pointed to the door.

Nick ignored him, glaring at Momma. "I'm serious."

If she caved and let Nick stay, Sam wasn't sure what he would do. Or what Momma would do to him. He hadn't ever stood up to her or for her like this before. Which one of them would she choose?

She nodded more forcefully this time. "I'm serious too. Go."

Nick spun on his heel and marched stiffly to the door. With one hand on the knob, he gave Momma an over-the-shoulder, raised eyebrow dare.

Sam glanced between them, praying that she would maintain her resolve.

She watched Nick, her hands fidgeting in front of her, but she remained silent.

After a long, painful pause, Nick growled something under his breath, wrenched the door open, and left.

Once his tires squealed out of the driveway, Momma let out a shuddering breath. So did Sam.

"I can't believe you did that," she said.

"What? Told him to leave? He's no good, Momma."

"I can take care of myself. No one asked you to come running in."

"I could hear him yelling from Mrs. Harris's yard. I'm sure other neighbors heard him too. There's no reason for him to talk to you like that." He squared his shoulders and stared her down, daring her to disagree. "I'm sure you can take care of yourself just fine, but having a little help isn't so bad either, is it?"

"I don't want to talk to you right now." Momma took one last look at the door and then marched down the stairs to her room.

Was she regretting making Nick leave? She'd said they were through, but Sam had a feeling that if she called him in an hour, he'd be back, giving her 'one last chance' or some other ridiculous line.

Sam let out a frustrated growl.

He considered following her downstairs to smooth things over, but Momma only said she didn't want to talk to him when she was really angry and trying to keep from exploding. He let her be. It wasn't that he'd expected her to be grateful for his bursting in, but in light of what Nick had broken and said, he didn't understand why she was so angry at him. She should be angry at Nick, for heaven's sake.

Sam grabbed the trashcan from the kitchen and brought it into the living room. Getting to his hands and knees, he began picking bits of glass out of the carpet. He'd just about finished and was going for the vacuum when Sianna got home.

She surveyed the remaining sparkling glass in the middle of the room. "What's all that?"

"Grandma's vase. Nick smashed it."

Sianna gasped. "Where is he? How's Momma?"

"I told him to leave. For good. Momma did too."

Sianna's mouth dropped open. "You didn't."

He nodded. "Like you wouldn't have done the same thing if you had walked in and heard what he called her."

"I don't even want to know." She tucked her hair behind her ears and crossed her arms over her chest.

Sam set the vacuum down. "What's wrong?"

he asked, noticing wet streaks on her cheeks now that her hair was out of her face.

"Nothing." She sighed and shook her head. "Paolo. We broke up."

His first reaction was relief. If she wasn't seeing the guy who made a hobby out of publicly groping his sister, maybe the rumors about her would die down. Maybe she'd take some time off from dating and focus on her grades. Momma wanted one of them to go to college. Going to jail would ruin his chances. That dream was going to fall to Sianna.

He mustered a sympathetic smile as he plugged in the vacuum. "Sorry to hear that. Want to talk about it?"

"No, but thanks." Sianna eyed the basement stairs. "How's Momma?"

"Mad at me. But I'll take that over her having anything to do with Nick."

Sianna nodded. "Me too. Well, not that I want her to be mad at you."

Sam smiled. Sianna always made him feel better. "Thanks. Hey, I'm going to church with the neighbors on Sunday. Do you want to come?"

He felt pretty confident that Mrs. Harris would be fine with Sianna tagging along. She probably wouldn't mind if Momma wanted to come too.

Sianna made a face. "Why?"

"Why not?"

"I'll pass. Maybe you can talk Momma into it?"

As mad as she was? Probably not. It would be better to give her some space until she was ready to talk.

"Do you need help with this?" Sianna asked, gesturing at the floor.

"No, I've got it."

"I'll go see about the other half of the mess then." She tipped her head toward the stairs.

"Good luck."

More likely, Sianna wanted to talk to Momma about Paolo, but maybe the two of them could console each other. He didn't know how Sianna could date as much as she did. Not after the stream of men like Nick that Momma brought home. That right there had been enough to make him swear off dating until after graduation. He didn't need that kind of aggravation to distract him from work and school. And now he wondered, would he ever date? With Aralim's task hanging over his head, he had a limited time before his future was a prison cell and an untimely death.

Sam pondered his immediate options. There were a couple of girls in school he could see himself asking out and maybe not getting immediately shot down. Would kissing Hailey Green or getting to any of the dating bases the guys bragged about with Sharice Jackson change his future? Would they make him feel any better about it?

He vacuumed up the glass dust while imagining spending time alone with Hailey and Sharice. Without a car and on limited funds, neither imaginary date went well. Maybe his life was complicated enough right now without trying to drag anyone else into it, no matter how temporarily.

He finished cleaning up the mess and put the vacuum away. The end table next to the worn couch looked bare without Grandma's vase.

Having eaten plenty of dinner with Henry, Sam wasn't hungry. He went to his room, closed the door, and turned out the light. If he didn't look at the Harris house and squeezed his eyes shut, he wouldn't know if Aralim was out there glaring at him.

He'd done his one good deed for the day. Surely that had to earn him a little favor with the demanding angel?

8

By Sunday morning, Momma was talking to him again, but only when she had to. The kind looks and soft smiles that assured him that all was right with the world, in as much as it could be, remained absent. To make matters worse, Sianna had been staying in her room since her talk with Momma. She didn't seem exactly mad at him, but she wasn't her usual sisterly-self either.

Buried in homework, Sam considered cancelling the church outing with Mrs. Harris and Henry. He looked at the pile of assignments he'd put off because of work and babysitting. And he had to work in the evening. And he wanted to maybe clean up the yard a little. The more time he spent next door sneaking glances out the side window, the more the mess his family had let go bothered him. If he could get a ladder out and find a hammer, he could at least fix the hanging gutter and maybe clean out the ones Mrs. Harris could see. Winter would be hitting soon and then everything would have to wait until Spring. With Aralim after him, who knew what Spring would hold? Or if he'd even be around.

He was just about to go out to the kitchen to call Mrs. Harris to cancel when it occurred to him that if he went to church even just this once, he might be able to start a conversation with Pastor Joe after the service without Momma hovering like she did when he brought food by. He could ask about Aralim, find out if he was a legit angel, and get some advice about what he should do in either case.

Sam surveyed his closet. He'd grown out of his Sunday best shortly after they'd stopped going to church. The pants and shirt he'd worn to the Sophomore homecoming dance, the last one he'd bothered to go to, were the closest thing he had. There had to be a tie around somewhere. He searched through his closet and found it on the floor. Thankfully, it wasn't wrinkled in the part that mattered.

After spending a good twenty minutes trying to remember how to tie the tie, he ducked into the bathroom to make sure he was presentable. Sianna put her brush down and started past him.

"You can stay," he offered. "I just wanted to make sure I didn't miss anything."

"You look fine," she said quietly.

The mirror confirmed that he hadn't missed a button and didn't have any of his breakfast lodged in his teeth. He ran his fingers through his hair, then noticed his shoes.

Sianna, leaning against the doorframe, followed his gaze. "Grow out of your dress shoes?"

"Yeah. Think anyone will notice my sneakers?"

"They're red. Yes, they're going to notice. But," she punched his arm softly, "screw them. They're in church. Not supposed to judge others, right?"

"There is that, I suppose." But he knew everyone did. That's why they'd stopped going. But, if he wanted to find a chance to talk to Pastor Joe, he would have to endure a few stares.

"I'll see you tonight. Have a good day, alright?" He hoped she would. He missed her jokes and smiles as much as Momma's.

"Sure. You too." She gave him a half-hearted smile and set her brush on the counter before heading back to her room.

Sam stopped by the top of the stairs as he passed through the kitchen to the living room. He called down, "Momma? I'm leaving for church. I'll be back later."

She muttered something he couldn't make out. Glad to leave the tension in the house behind, he headed out the front door and to the Harris' house.

"Go on, get in the car," Mrs. Harris said upon spotting him from where she sat on the porch. "Henry will be out in just a minute." She leaned into the house through the front door and hollered, "Come on. We're going to be late."

Mrs. Harris appeared more frazzled than she'd already been for the past couple of weeks. Her hair stood up in the back as though she'd forgotten to comb and curl the part she couldn't see. One eye had a thicker smear of eyeliner underneath than the other, and her skirt hung crooked under the edge of her long coat.

A chilly fall breeze kicked up, sending the first fallen leaves fluttering through the air. The wind picked up her hair in stiff clumps and swirled them around, putting her already questionable hairdo in total disarray. She let out a frustrated sound and patted her hair down. As if feeling how out of place everything was, she peered at the front window at her reflection.

"Well, isn't that just a fine mess," she said.

"It's not that bad." Sam quickly opened up the back door of her shiny blue car and slid inside. The seat and floor were spotless. The air inside smelled like new car. It wasn't. She'd had it since before her husband had died. How did she keep it smelling so nice? Momma's car smelled like cigarettes and old fries. He took a deep breath and settled into the comfortable seat. The seatbelt fit around him just right and didn't make any of the raspy, squeaky noises he was used to.

Henry came running out of the house like something was chasing him. Mrs. Harris grabbed his hand on his way past her, jerking him to a halt. She gave him a few stern words before they both walked to the car and got in. Henry climbed onto the booster seat next to him. Mrs. Harris clicked his seatbelt into place and then closed the door with more force than necessary. She got into the front and started the car. The radio blared a country song. Her hand shot to the dashboard and the music turned off.

They drove the three blocks to church in silence. Sam wanted to ask Henry what was going on, but he didn't dare with everything so quiet. He didn't want to get the kid in more trouble.

When they arrived at church, the parking lot was already mostly full. They had to park in the farthest row.

"Good thing I bothered to do my hair today," Mrs. Harris grumbled as they jogged to the front door.

Once they were safely out of the wind, she hung up her coat in the coatroom and then excused herself to the women's room for a moment.

Sam pulled Henry out of what was left of the milling crowd that hadn't yet filtered in to find a pew. "What's up this morning?" he asked.

"Momma's upset about Nana. She's in a bad mood."

"I noticed. Did something change with your Grandma?"

Henry nodded and his eyes grew wet. Sam patted his shoulder. "I didn't mean to make you sad."

Henry sniffed. "Momma said she's getting worse. That Nana forgot her name yesterday. She was real sad. Nana doesn't remember me either."

"I'm sorry." Sam didn't know what more to say. "Maybe we can say a prayer for her in church today?"

Henry's face perked up. "Yeah!"

Mrs. Harris reappeared, looking a bit more herself. "Let's find a seat, shall we?"

Pastor Joe stood by the entryway. His eyes grew wide as they approached. "Samuel Mason, it's good to see you! How's your mother?"

"Well enough, I suppose." Considering Momma wasn't really talking to him but was also thankfully not talking to Nick, he'd call it a win. However, not a very victorious one. He'd lost count of how many times he'd caught her staring at the empty side table where Grandma's vase had resided.

"That's good to hear. I'll try to bring her something special with your next food box. Maybe she'll join us one of these Sundays too?"

"Maybe." He tried to sound hopeful, but he knew she wouldn't. No amount of food bribery would get her back where people could talk about her in whispering range.

"Well, I'm glad you're here and I hope you enjoy the service."

Mrs. Harris led them into the sanctuary and down to one of the open pews in the middle. They sat on either side of Henry who looked happy to be between them. The seat was just as uncomfortable as Sam remembered.

As if summoned by a signal Sam couldn't see, the stragglers from outside came in and sat down. Pastor Joe followed behind the last of them and headed up to the pulpit. Once the opening prayer was started, the service melded into every other one that he remembered. They sang, and Pastor Joe talked about God and sin and forgiveness. He read a bible verse, but it didn't have anything to do with angels so Sam kind of tuned out. Instead of reading along with the bible that he held down to share with Henry as if Henry could read, Sam ended up gazing at the other attendees.

While there were some new members, most were familiar faces. He caught curious glances in his direction, along with covert whispering between couples.

Henry nudged him. Sam realized they were

supposed to be praying. He put the bible down on his lap and bowed his head, unsure if he dared continue his surveillance during the prayer or if that would make him look bad if he were caught by others doing the same thing. He decided to play it pious and kept his head down and eyes closed. Pastor Joe's voice droned on in an almost hypnotic cadence.

Sam had never been one for praying but he said a few silent words. *Mrs. Harris is already in a bad way. Surely you can't want her to lose Henry while she's taking care of her mother? Whatever you need Henry for elsewhere can wait, can't it?* He waited but God didn't answer.

Sam cracked an eyelid open, checking for any blinding light, but Aralim didn't make an appearance to chastise him either. Was anyone even listening? He wasn't sure if it made him feel better or worse that no one answered.

A resounding Amen filled the sanctuary. Sam lifted his head to see everyone starting to reach for their hymnbooks. He'd never been a big fan of singing, but at least when the organ started, he knew he could stand to stretch out and maybe wake up after the long prayer. Mrs. Harris found the song and gave the book to Henry to hold. He rested it on the back of the pew in front of them so all three of them could see the words. Henry mumbled along.

The first verse felt awkward, as if Sam's throat needed to remember how to sing along with everyone else. It seemed like his voice stood out no matter if he sang quieter or not. By the time the chorus kicked in, he'd found his place in the congregation. When the song ended, Henry left with the other children to go downstairs and then the sermon started in earnest.

When the service wrapped up, Sam was almost sad. It felt good to be part of something, of the group. He didn't remember that feeling when he'd been there before. Maybe he'd been too young to appreciate it.

Sam followed Mrs. Harris out to the big welcome room where two couples had coffee, milk, and cookies waiting for everyone. He got in line and made his selection: a chocolate chip cookie the size of his hand. Mrs. Harris took only coffee.

"You can have my cookie if you want. Or maybe bring one home for your sister?" she said over her shoulder.

Maybe a big cookie would cheer Sianna up. He found a peanut butter one and wrapped it in a napkin. The lady manning the table raised her eyebrow.

Mrs. Harris took one look at her and said, "I'm saving mine for later. Is that a problem?"

The lady, dressed in a floral dress and bright pink lipstick, smiled. "Of course not." But she watched Sam step away with the second cookie like he'd stolen a twenty out of her purse.

"Don't mind them," said Mrs. Harris. "I'm happy you're here." She urged him to follow her away from the tables. "Do you have anyone you'd like to talk to? Do you remember any of the kids you used to have Sunday school with or maybe someone from school?"

He'd never paid attention to how much time his parents had stood up here making their cup of coffee last while he'd recited his memorized verse of the week in return for a sticker. He'd been wrapped up in singing songs with the other kids and doing a quick lesson that was more fun than work.

Guessing Mrs. Harris had friends to talk to, he gave her an out. "Actually, I wanted to talk to Pastor Joe. I'll try to watch for when it's time to leave."

She nodded with a grateful smile and then headed for a semi-circle of chatting women. Sam made his way toward the door, looking for Pastor Joe. Spotting him by the coffee line, Sam headed that way.

9

Seeing him approach, Pastor Joe quickly wrapped up a conversation with one of the stern-faced deacons in a grey suit. The pastor's robes made him seem far less formal, though Sam guessed that really wasn't the case. Yet, they made him feel approachable in a way that a business suit didn't.

"Is there something I can help you with?" Pastor Joe asked. "You look like you have something on your mind and it isn't Mrs. McNalley's cookies because you've only had a few bites. I know how good those are."

Sam realized he'd forgotten all about the cookies in his hand. "Yes. Do you have a minute?"

"For you? Of course. How about we step over there?" Pastor Joe indicated an empty corner with the nod of his head.

They made their way through the knots of

conversation and took up residence in the corner where Sam could easily watch to make sure no one was encroaching to overhear them.

"This is going to sound weird, but I think I saw an angel."

Pastor Joe took a long sip of his coffee. "There are angels all around us. What leads you to believe you saw one specifically?"

Sam leaned closer to whisper, "It was glowing and had huge wings?"

"And where did this happen?"

"In my house. Well, it was outside first, but then it came in."

"I see." Pastor Joe shuffled his feet and switched his coffee from his left to right hand. "And did this angel speak to you?"

"Yes. It told me its name and that I had to do something. Something terrible."

"The angel told you to do something terrible?" Pastor Joe started to look through the crowd. "Maybe you should talk to Mr. Albertson. He might be better suited to help you."

"I don't need help. I need to know if what I saw was really an angel."

"We don't know what angels look like exactly. It's more of a concept than a physical reality. What you describe sounds like what we commonly think of when someone mentions angels. But people don't actually see them. At least I never have.

Maybe you're more fortunate than me?" He smiled, still searching the coffee-swilling congregation.

"If you knew what it asked me to do, you wouldn't be thinking you were fortunate."

"Something terrible, you say?" Pastor Joe made eye contact with someone and waved them over.

'Kill someone' was right on the tip of his tongue, but the way Pastor Joe was acting made him hold back. "Yes."

A grey-haired man stepped out of the crowd and regarded Pastor Joe and Sam with blatant curiosity. "Something I can help you with, Pastor?"

"This is Samuel Mason." Pastor Joe held out his hand. "Karl Albertson. I think perhaps the two of you should talk. Maybe you could set up an appointment?"

"For what?" asked Sam.

"I'm a psychologist. I work for the state. I think your mother is set up for benefits, right?" He spoke with a German accent, like in one of those old war movies.

"Yes?"

"Then you're all set." Mr. Albertson pulled out his phone. "When works for you?"

"I'm not sure what this is about. I'm fine." Sam backed away. Seeking out Mrs. Harris, he hurried toward her.

Coming here was a mistake.

Now Pastor Joe thought he was nuts and either he or Mr. Albertson were going to call his mother. She didn't need that kind of worry. He was fine.

Mrs. Harris was deep in conversation with four other women. Two of them noticed him approaching. Their eyes went directly to his shoes. They both looked at each other. Mrs. Harris turned to see what they were looking at.

"Henry should be up in fifteen minutes. You didn't finish your cookie."

"I'm not hungry. I'm going to wait outside if that's okay?"

"Sure, but it's cold out. You didn't bring a coat."

"I'll be fine."

Sam hurried out of the room and through the hallway that led around the sanctuary back to the door near where Mrs. Harris had parked. On the off chance she'd left it unlocked, he made his way out to the car but then didn't dare touch the handle. She had one of those newer cars. It probably had a security alarm. People were already talking about him inside. He didn't need the stupid alarm to go off to draw more attention to himself. With his luck, someone would think he was trying to steal it. Sam hurried back to the church where he tucked himself in between two pillars to get mostly out of the wind.

It seemed like an hour later when Mrs. Harris

finally made her way out with Henry in hand.

"You look half-frozen," she remarked upon spotting him.

"I'm fine. It's not so bad out here." He tried to keep his teeth chattering to a minimum as they made their way out to the car at Henry's pace.

She unlocked the doors when they got within twenty feet. Luckily, he hadn't tried them, he thought to himself. The interior of the car, filled with sunlight, felt so good. He sunk back against the plush seat and closed his eyes.

"Would you like to come back to the house for lunch?" asked Mrs. Harris. "If you have time before you have to go to work?"

"I should get home, but thank you. Maybe another time."

"I'm glad you came with us today. Pastor Joe seemed happy to see you."

"He was." But Sam didn't plan on going back any time soon. "Thanks for inviting me."

The ride home passed too quickly. Soon he was walking in the wind again and back into his house.

He set the peanut butter cookie on the counter and wrote Sianna's name on the napkin with a marker from the kitchen drawer. He broke his in half. Setting it on a paper towel, he wrote Momma next to it. Maybe the cookies would have better luck with winning affection back from the women of the house.

Sam retreated to his room with the last bites of his cookie, a peanut butter sandwich, and a glass of water. He'd just settled onto the edge of his bed with the glass tucked between his legs when light flared in his room.

"What did you hope to accomplish with that stunt today?" asked Aralim.

"Stunt? I went to church," Sam said, clutching his meal but considering throwing the glass at the angel. "Seems like something you'd encourage."

"Under other circumstances, perhaps." He shook his head. "You made a mess. Why can't you just do what is asked of you? Why must you make this harder than it needs to be?"

"Harder than killing an innocent little kid? Than ruining my life? Harder than knowing what this will do to my family?" Sam clutched the glass so hard that water sloshed onto his pants.

"Your task was not meant to be easy," Aralim scolded.

"I didn't ask for a task at all."

"You were chosen."

The angel was starting to sound like one of his teachers, always harping on him for the same things.

"Look, I didn't ask to be chosen. I didn't want to be chosen. I just want to get through school, graduate, and find a full-time job so I can help get the house fixed up and give my sister a chance at maybe going to community college because I won't ever get there. Is that too much to ask?"

Aralim glared at him. "For anyone else, no. But you were—"

Sam raised the glass and took aim. "Do not say chosen."

The angel crossed his arms over his chest and cocked his head. "Assaulting an angel is not wise."

"I'm sure it isn't, but really, will it make my life any worse at this point?"

Aralim sighed. "Finish your food. I only stopped in to check on you. And to remind you that waiting—"

"Isn't helping anyone. Yeah, you've said that before. But I'm in no hurry to commit murder. Call it exercising my free will."

The angel shook its head. "I told God that whole initiative was a bad idea."

"Bet God agrees with you, given what you've asked me to do."

A vengeful aura flared around Aralim. "Watch yourself."

Was lightning going to strike him any second? Sam eyed the ceiling warily. "Sorry," he whispered for good measure.

"Your father left a gun in his closet. If you're wondering how you could get this task done," the angel said offhandedly.

Sam's stomach dropped. He set the sandwich on the bed, no longer hungry. "There's a gun in the house? Momma never said a word about that. She hates guns."

"That's why your father kept it hidden. If you don't have to get close, to use your hands directly, maybe that will make your task easier?"

Maybe? Except he'd never used a gun. He'd never even touched one. Other than watching people shoot them on TV, he had no idea how to go about aiming or firing one. Was there ammunition somewhere? If his father were around, he could have asked him. Sadly, that wasn't an option. He'd never even called.

It was like his father had fallen off the face of the earth. His father didn't have any siblings and his parents had passed away when Sam was in fourth grade. Momma said she'd looked for him, but Sam didn't know if she'd tried very hard. Momma wasn't good at using the internet other than getting her email at the library now and then.

"If you're really an angel, can you tell me about my father? Where is he?"

"*If* I'm an angel?" Aralim snarled. "You doubt me?"

Giant feathered wings unfurled from the angel's back and shot through the walls of Sam's room for lack of space.

"Put those away! What if someone sees you!"

"They won't see me unless I want them to. That's how we angels work."

Sam didn't recall ever seeing paintings or drawings of an angel looking disgusted, but he now knew what that looked like. Why couldn't Aralim be one of those softly smiling angels with a warm glow? Instead, he was all hard midnight-driving-high-beam in the eyeballs and wrath.

"Are all angels like you?"

It was hard to believe it was possible, but Aralim appeared even more offended. "Master bedroom closet. Do your task."

The angel vanished.

With a heavy sigh, Sam headed out to the kitchen to take care of the remnants of his meal. All he could think about was how to get Sianna out of her room so that he could search the closet to see if Aralim was lying about the gun.

10

Sianna stayed after school to work on a project. Sam checked the clock. Momma was on her way home and Henry's bus would arrive in five minutes.

He crept into Sianna's room. With her twin bed in place of his parent's king, the space was very open. Though she did have more floor space than he did, she'd covered it in clothes and papers.

Momma nagged her constantly to clean up her room, but she claimed to know where everything was and since she got good grades, Momma kept her nagging to a friendly level. Sam tried not to step on anything and not look down. He didn't want to accidently spot his sister's underwear or anything else personal. He shuddered just thinking about it.

Sianna had filled what had been their parent's walk-in closet with thrift-store finds. He shook his head at the jam-packed mess. The girl did like her five-dollar fill-a-bag specials.

Where would his father hide a gun? His mother had taken up as much closet space as Sianna, so it had to be on a shelf or maybe on the floor? He eyed the couple shoeboxes in the corner. Picking one up, he opened it quickly, as if he expected a gun to pop out at him. A pair of glittery gold shoes lay nestled in white tissue paper. Probably something Sianna had worn to a dance or hoped to. The other three boxes also held shoes. He was running out of time.

Sam reached up on his tip-toes and felt around the top shelf above the clothing rack. He came away with nothing but a dusty hand.

If there wasn't a gun here, if Aralim was wrong, it would be much easier to discount everything the angel had said. But he had to be sure. Sam knelt down and eyed the wooden floor. In movies, people hid stuff under floorboards. But that was for old houses, wasn't it? Not cookie-cutter suburb houses.

Deciding it wouldn't hurt to try, he knelt down and tapped the floor in a few places.

"Are you home?" Momma called out from the entryway.

"Just getting ready to head over to watch Henry," he yelled, hoping she wouldn't notice his voice was coming from further down the hall than usual.

He tapped more frantically and was finally rewarded with a hollow sound. With his fingers pried under the edges of one of the laminate flooring strips, he was surprised when it lifted right up. Two panels were connected by a couple of narrow wooden pieces along the bottom side. He tipped the section up to find a shallow, hollow rectangle with a box inside. It occurred to him the space was just big enough for the small fire safe his mother had shown him in the basement—in case something happened to her. He shuddered thinking of the future Aralim had shown him.

He hesitantly reached in to pull aside the lid of the box. Just as Aralim had said, his father had a gun in the house. Was it a pistol or a revolver? He didn't know a thing about what made them different. It sat there, menacing in the hollow space in the floor, taunting him that not only had his father owned a gun, but he'd hidden it. He'd left it. And the angel had known it was there. Staring at the gun, he could no longer pretend that everything Aralim said wasn't also true.

Sam grimaced.

He reached into touch the cold metal but stopped short of picking up the gun. A smaller cardboard box sat next to the pistol. He flipped up the top to find a neat square of bullets all waiting in their rows. Just one of them could end a life. And there were so many.

Feeling sick to his stomach, Sam slid the flooring back into place and ducked out of Sianna's closet. He peeked out into the hallway, and hearing Momma in the kitchen, made a run for his room.

After gathering up his backpack, he sped through the kitchen to find Momma surveying the contents of the freezer. "I'll be back after eight. See you later." He planted a quick peck on her cheek.

"You're always gone these days, aren't you? Always on the run."

"Staying busy," he said.

"You better be staying out of trouble. Pastor Joe called the other day.

Sam's feet seemed to stick to the floor. "What did he want?"

"I think you know full well. And some Mr. Albertson, with a German accent, he called too. He was concerned about you. Some business with angels?"

"Just a weird dream I had. They misunderstood," he said quickly. "I'm fine, Momma. I've got to go."

"Mr. Albertson wants you to make an appointment. After the call I got—which why does everyone expect that I check my email every blessed day—from your math teacher, I'm thinking a talk with someone other than me might be a good idea. I told him you'd check your work schedule and return his call. The number is on the fridge."

"I don't need to talk to anyone," he grumbled as he walked out the door.

"You better make that call!" Momma shouted

after him just as the front door closed.

Fat chance of that happening. Aralim had been right. He shouldn't have said anything.

The bus was waiting in front of the neighbor's house. Sam hurried over and waved at the driver through the open door.

"You're late. Please make an effort to be on time. We have a schedule to keep."

"Sorry, I will." Sam waved to Henry, urging him to walk faster as he came down the aisle and down the steps.

When Henry hit the driveway, his steps moved no faster and he dragged his backpack behind him.

"What's up, little man?"

"Nothing," he mumbled. "Let's just go in."

Sam took Henry's backpack and added it to his other shoulder. He followed as Henry trudged up the porch stairs and waited patiently while Henry pulled the chain out from under his shirt to expose the house key. He set to unlocking the door.

"You want help with that?"

"I can do it. I'm not a baby."

"Didn't say you were." Sam took a step back and let Henry fumble a bit before finally getting the door unlocked and opened. He went inside without holding the door open like he usually did.

"Rough day at school?" Sam couldn't remember much of his own kindergarten year. Most of it was a blur of carefree days on the playground, snacks, and rose-cheeked Mrs. Herna with her long white braid and big smile. For a second, he could feel her thick, nubby grey sweater against his cheek when she gave him her usual morning hug. Now teachers weren't allowed to do that, no touching other than maybe a handshake. It didn't seem right.

Henry grunted.

"Did that Mikayla girl give you trouble again?" he tried, sensing he was maybe onto something.

"She was awful, like every day. She tried to steal my cupcake. Momma made it special for me." From the narrowed eyes and pursed lips, it was clear Henry wasn't going to forgive Mikayla anytime soon. "But mostly it was Harrison Albertson."

Sam went cold. "What did he do?" he asked.

"He said that you're crazy. That you're bad. Nuts in the head. His dad said so. Says you're gonna hurt someone or do something bad. I told him he was the nutso one."

Sam patted Henry on the shoulder. "Thanks, little man. His dad should keep his mouth shut. He misunderstood something I was trying to talk to Pastor Joe about. They both got it all wrong."

"I know you're not nuts in the head." Henry beamed up at him. "But he made me so mad."

"Was that the end of it? You just told him he was the crazy one? Tell me that was the end." But his gut said it wasn't.

"I kicked him. We were on the playground.

The aide saw. She put me on the timeout bench. It was the long recess too. And it was cold just sitting there with everyone staring at me."

"I'm sorry you had to miss out on your recess and that kids were staring at you."

"Momma's gonna be mad." He reached for his backpack.

Sam set it down on one of the chairs by the table along with his own.

Henry unzipped his and rifled through the contents. He pulled out a pink paper. "See, I have to get this signed and turn it in tomorrow or else I have to go sit in the office for all of the recesses until I do."

For a moment, Sam considered forging Mrs. Harris's signature to save Henry the scene with his mother, but his conscience wouldn't let him. Instead, he took the paper and set it on the counter. He'd talk to Mrs. Harris, try to soften her up a little. That was the least he could do.

"You hungry?" he asked, hoping to take Henry's mind off the paper.

"No. I just wanna go watch TV."

"You know you're supposed to do your homework first. How about we sit down and do homework together?"

"Can Squidman help?"

"Sure. Go get him."

Henry went up the stairs at a more normal

pace and returned ten minutes later looking just as glum as when he'd walked off the bus.

"Can't find him?"

"No, and I looked everywhere."

Sam held out his hand. "Let's look together."

It took three minutes for Sam to spot the missing action figure on Henry's dresser. Mrs. Harris must have set it up there out of sight from below.

"Thanks!" Henry grinned and ran for the stairs.

Sam had just turned off the bedroom light when a loud crash followed by a piercing wail made his heart jump into his throat.

"Henry!" Sam raced to the stairs.

Henry lay halfway down on his stomach, his head against the railing with blood trickling down from a cut over his eyebrow. Tears ran down his red face as he looked up to Sam.

Please don't let it be anything serious, Sam begged whoever might be listening. Mrs. Harris was going to be really mad if something happened to her son on his watch.

"Are you alright?" he asked hesitantly. That cut was going to be impossible to cover up.

"My arm hurts." Henry tried to move, but he yelled again and stayed put.

"Oh Lord, I hope you didn't break it." He cringed, already imagining the tirade that would be heading his way.

"I don't know," Henry blubbered.

He'd deal with Mrs. Harris later. Henry needed him right now. Sam slid onto the step beside Henry and helped sit him up. The boy kept his arm close to his chest.

"Can you move it?"

"It hurts too much."

"Show me where."

Henry wiped his runny nose on his sleeve and then paled when he saw the blood on his sleeve from his cut. He pointed near his wrist with shaking fingers.

"Let's go clean up that cut and put some ice on your arm. Then I better call your mom."

Sam held Henry's good hand. "Why don't you sit on the couch for now. Maybe lay down? I'll get the ice."

"Momma has an icepack in the freezer. It's blue."

Sam didn't have to dig far into the freezer to find it. The pliable ice pack looked to be from a chiropractor's office. He'd never been to one of those. He'd barely been to the regular doctor. Momma only took him when he needed shots growing up, and only because school required it.

He brought a damp paper towel, the ice pack, and a dishtowel to wrap it in. After cleaning up the cut, which was thankfully small, he had Henry hold the paper towel in place to keep pressure on it. While he was busy, Sam settled the wrapped icepack onto Henry's already swelling arm. Now he had to call Mrs. Harris. The thought made him cringe.

"I'll be right back," he said.

Sam hurried to the kitchen and called the number Mrs. Harris had left by the phone. He'd not had to use it before and it felt weird to use it now, probably because it was a call he really didn't want to make.

A woman answered. Not knowing if it was her cell number or the number at her mother's house, he said, "Mrs. Harris?"

"Sam? Is Henry okay?"

"Sorry, no. He fell on the stairs. I think he may have broken his arm."

Mrs. Harris gasped. "Is he okay? I mean, I know he's not, but is he in a lot of pain? Where is he? Can I talk to him?"

"He's on the couch. I put ice on it, but I think he should go to the emergency room."

"One moment." The sound on the other end grew muffled. "Mom, it's Henry. He may have broken his arm. No, I can't leave you alone. No. Mom, you're not supposed to be alone."

"Mrs. Harris?" Sam said, hoping she could hear him.

"What is it, Sam?" she sounded angry.

He winced. "I'm really sorry. Maybe I can

have my mother drive us to the urgent care so you can stay there? I can sit in back with Henry so he's not scared."

The line went quiet a moment. When she came back to the phone, she sounded less agitated. "That would be very helpful, Sam. Please call me back after you talk to your mother, alright?"

"I will. Bye."

He quickly dialed home and waited. The phone rang and rang. He glanced out the window. The car was in the driveway. The answering machine picked up.

"Momma, pick up the phone." He hung up and counted to ten, then dialed again.

This time, she picked up. "What are you doing calling? Why don't you just come home if you need something. I'm just running a bath so I'm not gonna bring you anything right this instant."

"Momma, I need you to get dressed and take Henry and I to the hospital. I think he broke his arm and Mrs. Harris can't come home right now."

"That's just great, Samuel. Just great. What if she sues us? Do you have his insurance information? We certainly can't pay for any of this."

"We'll figure it out. Can you take us?"

"Don't really have a choice, do I?" She sounded even more annoyed than Mrs. Harris. "So much for my quiet night at home."

"Momma."

"Yes, fine. I'll be over in a minute. I want to take a look at this arm before we go running off. If you're exaggerating... I really don't need this, Sam."

"I know. Thank you."

Sam hung up the phone before she could say anything else to make him feel worse. He went back into the living room.

"How's your arm?" he asked, considering whether to lift up the ice pack to take a look.

"It hurts." Henry's lip quivered.

"My mother is on her way over to take a look. She'll bring us to a doctor. I better call your mom back. You good for a minute more?"

Henry nodded, but looked like he wanted to say no.

Sam hurried back into the kitchen and called Mrs. Harris to let her know what was going on.

"Take him straight to the emergency room, Sam. Don't waste time on that urgent care center. There's a folder by the refrigerator with an insurance card. Give them my number to call for authorization. Is that clear?"

"Yes, ma'am."

She hung up without even saying goodbye.

"Let me in," Momma said as she pounded on the front door.

Sam went to the entryway and unlocked the door. Mrs. Harris insisted that it remained locked at all times. He wasn't sure what kind of neighborhood she thought they all lived in. It wasn't like they were downtown in the blocks where the cops spent most their time. They barely saw cops drive by here, let alone stop anywhere.

"Where is he?" Momma demanded.

Sam led her to the couch in the living room.

Momma leaned over Henry's arm and picked up the ice pack. "Oh good Lord! Yes, that's broken. Come on." She let out a long-suffering sigh.

"Where's your coat?" Momma asked.

Sam wasn't sure which of them she was asking, but he grabbed both his and Henry's coats from the backs of the kitchen chairs. After putting his on, he helped Henry sit up. "Let's just put this around your shoulders."

Momma went to the front door, looking annoyed for having to wait for them. "Well, come on."

Once they got in the car, she took off with a jarring lurch. Her car stuck in gear sometimes. Someday, maybe she'd get it fixed. Sam held onto Henry, glad he was staying mostly calm. Though, he imagined that if his mom was there, he'd probably be crying. Something about being with strangers made it easier to keep the hurt inside. Not that he was a stranger anymore, but Momma was, and she wasn't being super nice about any of this. Then again, she'd never been all that friendly around kids, especially not when he or Sianna had friends over.

They made it to the emergency room in record time. Momma may have run a stop sign and he was pretty sure two of the stoplights had been what she called 'orange' as they passed underneath.

"You two get inside. I'll park the car and come find you."

Sam's fingers wrapped around the insurance paper and Henry's hand.

"I want my mom," Henry whispered.

"She'll be here as soon as she can. She's busy with your grandma. Truth be told, she sounded like she'd much rather be here with you." He squeezed Henry's hand.

A nurse met them at the door. She took them to a waiting room and then asked Sam a bunch of questions that all seemed to blur together.

"I have his insurance card and his mother's phone number." He offered her the card and a piece of paper.

The nurse took them and then handed him a pen and clipboard. "Fill this out. Someone will be with you shortly."

Sam sat beside Henry, who was now clutching his arm to his chest under his coat. "We shouldn't have to wait long."

He got to work filling out the long form. He wished he had a cell phone so he could ask Mrs. Harris the answers to all the blanks he didn't know.

A few more weeks of saving and maybe he could get one of those family phone bundles. Sianna wasn't the only one who could use a phone of her own.

He'd just finished what he could and set the clip board down when Momma came in. Her face was drawn and lips in a tight line. She stalked over and slammed her purse down into the seat next to Sam.

"You owe me, boy. I got a ticket. A flipping cop was following us through that last light."

He couldn't see how that was his fault. He certainly hadn't been driving, but he kept his mouth shut.

"Now I have a ticket to pay. I really didn't need this, Samuel. Really didn't. I wanted a hot bath. Just a simple quiet night." She dropped into a seat one over from him, keeping her purse planted between them.

Henry glanced in her direction, with tears welling in his eyes.

"It's okay, little man. Don't worry about it." He wrapped his arm around Henry and gave him a gentle squeeze like he remembered his father doing to him when he was young. It struck him that he didn't recall what had changed or when, but there had been a time when his father had been involved with his life, like he had really cared back then. How did someone just turn that off? Could anyone turn that off? Just stop caring?

Was that what Aralim needed him to do?

"Henry Harris?" called a different nurse.

Sam stood up. Henry did too. Momma did not.

"I'll wait here, unless you need me?" she said, sounding like she did not want to be needed.

"I guess we can take care of this," Sam said uncertainly.

"You're eighteen. About time you learned. I'll be right here if you run into something you can't handle." Momma picked at her bright red fingernails. "When I was your age, I was pregnant, graduated, and house shopping with your father. My mother certainly wasn't driving me around."

From what he recalled hearing, Grandma had kicked Momma out for being pregnant at eighteen. Lucky his father was five years older and had a good job or they never would have ended up in the suburbs. He could have been living down in cop land. Sam shook his head and took Henry's hand as they followed the nurse deeper into the hospital.

The emergency room was a bustling mess of people coughing, a baby screaming, two different people moaning, and someone loudly vomiting. Henry stuck close.

The nurse led them to a bed and pulled a curtain around them. "You can put your coat on the chair there and then let's get you up on the bed. Sam took Henry's coat and sat in the beside chair.

The next two hours blurred together. A doctor stopped in twice. They took Henry out for an Xray and then brought him back. Several nurses, both men and women, went in and out. Now sporting a cast and his arm in a sling, Henry slid off the bed with Sam's help.

"Can we go home now? Will Momma be home?" Henry's eyelids hung low. They'd given him pain medication and said it might make him sleepy.

Sam checked the clock. "She should be home soon, if she's not already. She had to wait for your Grandma's night nurse to get there."

"Will you stay until she gets home? I'm tired."

"Of course. Like I'd leave you alone?"

A faint smile passed over Henry's face.

They followed another nurse back out to the lobby where Momma was waiting. She had her face buried in a magazine.

"Momma? We're all done here."

"It's about time." She glanced at Henry, her tone softening a fraction. "How's that arm?"

"It hurts a little less."

"Probably gave you something good for that." She chuckled. "Let's get you home so I can try that bath again."

They rode home in silence. Momma stopped at all the yellow lights and the stop signs. She pulled into the Harris' driveway and let them out.

"I'll see you at home," she said to Sam. "You'll be paying this ticket." She handed the long slip of paper to him.

A hundred and fifty dollars. Sam sighed. He'd need to work another week before he could even start thinking about getting a cell phone of his own. It occurred to him that he had to start thinking about Christmas too. It was less than two months away, and if he didn't buy gifts, they'd be stuck with whatever dollar store finds Momma picked up. Sianna never had money so she usually made them something.

Childhood Christmases had always seemed so magical. Like a grand adventure every year. There had been presents under the tree, all wrapped up in shiny paper with ribbons and bows. They hadn't set up a tree in years now. He hoped Henry had Christmases like he used to, even though his father wasn't around. Mrs. Harris seemed the kind of mom to make frosted cookies and sing songs while decorating the tree. She probably had color-coordinated gift wrap and bows. He chuckled to himself as he used Henry's key to let them in.

Shoving the ticket that wasn't his into his pocket, Sam went about helping Henry up the stairs and then getting his shirt off.

"You got a good bruise on your forehead too. Those stairs put up one heck of a fight," Sam said.

Henry laughed sleepily.

"Do you want something to eat before you go to bed? Are you thirsty?"

"One of the nurses gave me crackers and juice."

Sam's stomach rumbled. "Okay, I'll turn out the light but keep your door open. I'll be downstairs until your mom comes home. Yell if you need anything."

Mrs. Harris made it home by eight. She tore into the driveway and was in the garage as soon as the door cleared the roof of the car. She burst through the door and into the kitchen.

"Where is he?"

"In bed. The pain meds made him sleepy. Again, I'm really sorry about this."

She waved a hand at him, already headed for the stairs. "We'll talk about it tomorrow. Thank your mother for getting him to the hospital."

"I will."

Mrs. Harris didn't look back. She hurried up the stairs and disappeared.

The way she'd said they'd talk about it made his stomach flip flop. He glanced at the pink paper on the counter and groaned. So much for talking to Mrs. Harris about that.

He slipped his coat on and headed home. The lights were all out upstairs when he walked in the front door.

"Momma?"

She yelled up the stairs, "We'll talk tomorrow,

Samuel. You make sure you get your homework done. And you better call Mr. Albertson. He called again."

Sam heaved a sigh, sloughed off his shoes and went to his room. Tomorrow was going to suck, he just knew it.

Sam's day started with riding his bike to school in the rain. Second hour, his algebra teacher kept him after class to talk about his near failing grade. In fifth hour, his biology teacher returned the essays from the week before with an F and a 'please see me after school' in big red letters across the top.

Since it was still raining after school, he was in no hurry to get home. Sam returned to his biology teacher only to find Mrs. Hanson, the assistant principal, also waiting there for him.

"Why don't you have a seat?" his teacher said, pointing to the front and center chair.

Sam sat, putting his backpack on the floor beside him. "I thought I did okay on this one. What did I do wrong this time?"

"You didn't follow instructions. Did you even read them?" asked the teacher.

He was pretty sure he had. How much

instruction did writing an essay on a biology topic off a list did a person need?

"You were supposed to write a paper with a classmate. Five pages. With your sources listed properly at the end."

He didn't remember seeing any of that. Or hearing her mention it. "When did you tell us that?"

"In class." She shook her head.

"I've been talking to your teachers," said Mrs. Hanson. "We follow up on any of our students that are in danger of not graduating. We care about you, Samuel. We want you to be successful."

The teacher sat at her desk while the assistant principal came closer to lean down only a few feet from him. "You're not failing your classes *yet*, but one C and all D's is too close for comfort. You're almost there. You just need to pay more attention to directions. If you need afterschool help, we're here for you. All you have to do is ask."

"I can't stay after school most of the time. I have a job. Two of them lately."

"You should be focusing on school. Jobs can wait until after graduation."

"The grocery bill can't wait that long. I need electric so I can see to do homework," he snapped. Did they really think that all kids had two parents supporting their family income? He knew plenty of kids who were in similar situations to his, or that only had one working parent, or were just holding on to their houses. "Not everyone is as fortunate as you."

"No one implied that you were unfortunate," Mrs. Hanson said carefully. "What I mean to say is that we want you to focus on school while you're in school."

"Sure," Sam said, not at all happy about the conversation.

"Alright then, I think we've covered enough for now. I've left a message with your mother. I'd like to set up a meeting with her and you together. It would be beneficial to have us all on the same page, I think."

"She's sick of all of you bothering her at work."

The assistant principal held up her hand. "I left a message at home. We don't have a cell number on file for her."

"She doesn't have one. None of us do. They're expensive."

"I see. There are programs that can help with the cost. I can provide that information in our meeting."

"She doesn't like handouts."

Mrs. Hanson smiled tightly. "Thank you for meeting with us, Samuel. I'll notify you of the time for our family meeting when I hear from your mother."

He knew he should say something, be polite and respectful, but he was too angry to give in to his mother's nagging voice in his head. She'd be angry too. She already was from yesterday.

As he got up, grabbed his backpack, and walked out of the room, he wished he'd brought his uniform to school so he could just go straight to work. There was no way he'd make it home before her now that he'd stayed after.

Feeling ready to burst, Sam unlocked his bike and took his time pedaling home.

He walked in the door to find Momma having a cup of coffee with Mrs. Harris. Henry sat on the couch with Squidman and a pile of green army men, enacting a battle.

"Hey, little man."

Henry turned and smiled. "Hi, Sam."

"How did it go with the pink paper?" he asked quietly.

Henry shook his head, his smile vanishing. "Not good."

"About time you're home. Where have you been?" scolded Momma.

Sam headed toward the kitchen. "I had to stay after to talk to the assistant principal."

"That nosey Mrs. Hanson?" Momma rolled her eyes. "Yeah, she called. We'll talk about that later. Right now, how about you have a seat at the table with us?"

With his stomach about dragging on the floor, Sam made his way to the table and sat down across from Mrs. Harris. She was dressed all nice, like she was going to a business meeting.

"He's all yours," Momma said like she was offering him up.

Mrs. Harris rubbed her fingers together and licked her lips. "While I appreciate what you did for Henry yesterday, the taking care of him at the hospital part, I'm concerned about your lack of properly watching him at my home."

"I..." What could he say? He thought he had been, but unless he held Henry's hand all the time, it was unlikely he could have prevented his fall.

"I know this was an accident," she said. "But I can't help but feel that if I had been there, he wouldn't have been running down the stairs."

He nodded numbly. He couldn't argue with that. Henry wouldn't have dared run on the stairs if she had been home. Sam tried to be good about following her rules. Henry also followed them when she wasn't there. Except this one time. And now he had a broken arm on Sam's watch.

"I'm really sorry," he said quietly.

"I know, and I appreciate all you've done. You've been a great help. Until yesterday."

Sam cringed. Did she have to drive that comment home like a dagger?

"In talking to your mother, it sounds like I've been taking too much of your time. You need to study. Graduation is important, Sam. I hope you'll devote the proper amount of attention to your studies."

"I'm trying," he said desperately. It wasn't like he was not turning assignments in on purpose. Sometimes teachers just didn't allow for enough time to do them. They didn't take students who had jobs into consideration. He couldn't always throw together a five-page essay in two days, not when he had back-to-back shifts between work and Henry.

He glanced at the couch where Henry was now staring over the back at them all. He held Squidman clutched in his hand.

"I know you're trying," said Mrs. Harris. "I should have realized you were already stretched thin. You have responsibilities here. I'll be adjusting my caregiver schedule for my mother so I can take Henry with me from now on."

"You don't have to do that. I—"

"It's already been decided," Momma announced.

Mrs. Harris slid four folded over twenty-dollar bills toward him. "With everything that happened, I forgot to pay you for last night."

"You don't have to pay—"

Mrs. Harris smiled sadly and shook her head. "Take it, Sam. It's yours."

As angry as he wanted to be over her cutting off his second income, he didn't have the heart for it. Taking her money now, no matter that he did really need it thanks to Momma's traffic ticket, felt wrong. He was about to argue further when she pushed the money closer, her eyes begging him to take it.

With a heavy sigh, Sam closed his fingers around the last of the cash he'd ever see from Mrs. Harris. He kissed his dream of a family phone plan goodbye.

"Now, you have work tonight. Why don't you get started on your homework before you head out in an hour." Momma pointed him toward his room.

She hadn't dismissed him like that since he was in his last year of elementary school. Was she trying to embarrass him to death?

With his face burning, Sam grabbed his backpack and started toward his room.

"Mom, I want Sam," whined Henry. "He's my friend."

Mrs. Harris pushed her coffee cup toward the center of the table and stood. "Sam has school work to do, honey. It's time to go. Why don't you say goodbye?"

Henry slid off the couch and ran to Sam, wrapping his good arm around Sam's legs. Sam ruffled his hair. "Goodbye, little man. You be careful on the stairs, okay?"

Henry nodded against his leg. "Sam?"

Sam looked down into Henry's teary brown eyes. "Yeah?"

"You can have Squidman. He can help you with your homework so you can come play with me again." Henry pressed the plastic action figure into Sam's hand.

Sam bent down and hugged Henry, his throat thick. "Thanks. I'll see you soon, okay?"

Henry nodded and then went to take his mother's waiting hand. Mrs. Harris gave Sam a nod before taking Henry out the front door.

He watched it close through blurry eyes.

"Since you're still out here," Momma said, thrusting her hands onto her hips. "Would you like to explain why you're nearly failing all your classes?"

"I'm trying, Momma. It's hard with work and trying to do things around here."

"It doesn't sound like you're trying very hard." She shook her head. "This is your senior year. You need to graduate. No dropout kid is living under my roof, you hear me?"

"I'm not dropping out, Momma. I'm trying to do my school work, honest. It's just—"

She waved a finger at him. "It's *just* sounding like you're about to make an excuse."

What did she want him to say? That it was her fault for not being able to pay all the bills? Maybe it was his father's fault for bailing on them? Or was it Sianna's fault for making him want to help provide for her in the hopes she'd be better at school than he was? All of that was true. Part of him wanted to yell it in her face. But he didn't.

"I'm sorry, Momma. I'll try harder."

"Damn right you will." She let out a huff. "Hand over that cash and the ticket you made me get. I'll need another seventy to cover the rest."

He dug around in his coat pocket to hand her the ticket and his pay. A quick trip to his bedroom and a dip into his cash stash later, he handed her the rest.

She nodded. "Bring home something for dinner after your shift tonight, will you? I have a craving for fries."

"Sure."

She leaned over and gave him a hug. "I know you're trying, Sam. Just do better, okay?"

Her arms around his shoulders made him feel solid, whole. Losing Henry and the babysitting job hurt a little less. Not much, but a little. Squidman's pointy little fingers dug into Sam's palm. He loosened his grip.

The only one who was going to be happy with this situation was Aralim. He could already hear the angel nagging him to complete his task. The line of people after him today was already long enough.

Momma put her hands on his shoulders and pushed herself away from him. She cleared her throat loudly. "Alright then, go on."

Sam went to his room and, after closing the door, flopped down onto his bed. Rather than pulling his homework from his backpack, he closed his eyes and wished the world and everyone in it, far away. But when he opened his eyes, everything was just as it had been. At least Aralim hadn't shown up.

Sam drifted off in his mind, seeing Henry's face and hearing his laugh. He'd always wanted a little brother. Sianna had adequately filled the sibling role but he realized after hanging out with Henry these past few weeks, a little brother would have been different. He squeezed the action figure still in his hand.

Now that was over. He'd screwed up. Or at least Mrs. Harris and Momma thought he had. In his heart, he didn't think he could have done anything differently. What had happened was between Henry and the stairs. It wasn't like he'd pushed Henry or told him to run. It was just an accident. But Mrs. Harris didn't see it that way or didn't want to. He had a feeling no amount of tears or whining from Henry was going to change her mind. She seemed like a determined kind of woman.

Was it an accident? Was it Henry's free will choice to run? Or had this been part of Aralim's warning that things would be worse for everyone the longer he waited? Sam rubbed his free hand over his face. Mrs. Harris would now be even more stressed having to rearrange her care schedule around Henry getting home from school. Henry had a broken arm. Now Sam knew them both so much better and he was still going to have to fulfill his task. He pondered the action figure in his hand. Why couldn't he just be a heartless villain like Squidman fought in the cartoons? Because cartoons weren't real, he explained to his aching conscience. Real life hurt.

Sam sat up and set Squidman on the bedside table next to the lamp that hadn't had a working light bulb in a year or two. Not that they didn't have light bulbs, it just hadn't been a priority to change it. Work, that's what he was supposed to be getting ready for. While he did have a nice stash of cash from Mrs. Harris, he was now going to have to make that last until Christmas and get back to relying on his regular job to help pay the bills.

He groaned, thinking of another shift of making fries, flipping burgers, or maybe getting a break and running the drive-thru instead. Sam sat up with a start, realizing that having stayed after school, the talk with Mrs. Harris, and now screwing around doing nothing, had eaten up more time than he'd realized. He was going to have to pedal fast and hope for light traffic if he was going to make it to work on time.

He changed into his uniform and threw on

his heavy hoodie and a coat. Momma was sitting at the kitchen table with a steaming cup of coffee in her hand.

"I don't suppose you could give me a ride?" he asked, knowing it was a long shot.

Momma shook her head. "I've got a date tonight. Since you chased Nick off, I had to find another man. He's a good one though, don't you worry."

Sam doubted it. She had terrible taste in men. He didn't remember his father being like Nick, or like any of the other long line of random guys she'd brought home that didn't treat her very well. Then again, his father had left her with two kids and not a single word. So maybe he was just as bad.

"Have a good night then." He gave her a quick kiss on the cheek and dashed out the door for his bike.

When he arrived at work, flushed and sliding his card into the time clock two minutes late while cramming his hat on, he spotted his manager shaking his head. He made a beeline for Sam.

"You're late."

"Traffic. Sorry. I'll try to be more on time."

"This isn't the first time, Sam. I know you're on a bike, but I can't keep making excuses for you. It's not fair to everyone else who does show up on time and is at their station when their shift starts."

"I know. I'm sorry." He'd already lost one job

today. He couldn't afford to lose another one.

"Don't make me warn you again. You're on drive-thru tonight."

Sam nodded as contritely as he could manage.

He hurried to the drive-thru window, feeling the heavy weight of Aralim's warning settle onto his shoulders.

12

Sam sat on the couch, knowing he should be working on his mid-semester civics paper but stuck on what topic to pick from the list. They all seemed so vague, nothing grabbed his attention. He turned on the TV in the hopes that the evening news might offer some inspiration.

A reporter with slicked back hair and a blue suit performed a bland-voiced, dead-eyed delivery of the news of a nine-year-old girl who had been found dead in a field in the nearby city of Georgetown. He supposed having to repeat stuff like that every day must eat at a person, that they might become immune to the horror of it all. The camera panned to a woman in a too-tight blouse and glaring gold necklace who went on about a flood in some foreign country and the death toll that was now in the hundreds.

Did God need all those souls elsewhere too? Or was this a free will thing that meant people were just in the wrong place at the wrong time? Had someone like him killed that little girl? Had it been an act of evil or someone following orders from an angel? Did they get a better deal than he had? They hadn't been caught yet. In fact, the police had little to go on. They were asking for help, for anyone to call in with tips. Was the killer going to get away with no consequences?

Aralim had been quite clear that he would be facing consequences. It wasn't fair that someone else could get away with murder when he couldn't. Not even on a murder he didn't want to commit.

Sam sank into the couch as far as he was physically able. He clutched one of the two pillows with frayed seams. Momma knew how to sew but she never seemed to get around to mending the gaping holes where filling poked out.

Was this what the weave of man looked like to God? Was he a needle and thread to sew up one of the frayed spots?

The pillow smelled musty and maybe like stale popcorn, reminding him of when he was younger. Friday nights had been family time, watching whatever old movie was on TV on this same couch with popcorn and soda. Momma didn't even buy popcorn anymore, and he couldn't recall the last time the three of them had sat on the couch together to watch anything.

He tossed the pillow aside.

The doorbell rang.

Momma was out on a date with some guy she hadn't deemed worthy enough to bring home for introductions yet. Sianna was seeing some new guy, someone from the football team this time. She'd moved on. Sort of.

Alone in the house, he checked the peephole and grimaced. The TV was on loud enough that anyone standing on the front step would know someone was home. Unfortunately.

He opened the door to Pastor Joe and Mr. Albertson.

Pastor Joe smiled widely. "Samuel. Just who we were hoping to see. May we come in?" He held a box in his arms. It looked heavy from the way the he shifted the weight onto one hip.

"Sure, I guess." He held the door open.

The two of them walked inside. Mr. Albertson shed his coat and handed it to Sam. Momma hung guest coats in the closet in the entry way. He supposed that was his duty since he was home alone. He hung up the coat and waited for Pastor Joe to take off his, but he didn't.

"We won't be too long," he said. "We just wanted to drop off some supplies for your family. With Thanksgiving next week, I thought you could use a little extra. Are you having family over?"

Momma hadn't mentioned having anyone visit. She didn't speak to her sister or her parents, and with his father's side of the family out of the picture, that left whatever guy she might be dating. He'd prefer to just have a quiet meal with the three of them.

"I don't know yet."

Sam took the box Pastor Joe offered him and found that it was indeed heavy. He brought it into the kitchen and put it on the counter. A bunch of red apples inside caught his eye. He could almost taste warm apple pie with vanilla ice cream on top. A true feast indeed.

"We wanted to have a talk with you about what you said at church a few weeks ago," said Mr. Albertson as he took a seat at the kitchen table without any invitation.

Pastor Joe also sat. Sam remained standing for a moment but then everything felt strained and awkward. Reluctantly, he pulled out a chair and joined them. Why couldn't they have picked an afternoon when he had to run off to work?

A yellow bus out the kitchen window caught his attention. Henry was home. But it wasn't his job to meet him at the bus anymore.

Mrs. Harris with her coat on and purse in hand, hurried out the front door and down the porch to meet the bus. They'd be leaving for Nana care duty as soon as she could get Henry in the car. No more hour of homework, snacks, or TV time, just long evenings doing whatever was available at his grandmother's house while his mom spent her time taking care of her mother. That didn't sound fair to Henry at all. Especially if the poor kid's days were numbered. He deserved to play and enjoy himself every minute he could.

With a sigh, Sam turned back to his unwelcome guests. "I was having a bad day. Everything is fine now."

"You said you were going to do something terrible," said Mr. Albertson, as if Sam hadn't said anything at all. "Can you tell me what you thought that might be?"

"I was wrong. I'm fine."

Pastor Joe gave him one of those patient, sad smiles that he normally saved for Momma. "It's okay to have a bad day, Samuel. It's also okay to feel lost or alone or like maybe you have a lot on your shoulders. More than a boy your age should, I mean."

While he didn't really want to talk to either of them, he knew they wouldn't leave until he'd divulged something, until they'd felt like they'd helped. That's what Pastor Joe did, after all, or tried to do.

"I've been having a hard time at school. And then Momma and my sister both had a bad breakup the same day. It was a lot to take in."

Mr. Albertson nodded. He pulled out a little notebook and a pen from his shirt pocket and jotted down a couple of lines. The way he held the notebook, Sam couldn't see what he was writing.

"Can you tell me what you thought you might do because you were having a bad day? It can be anything. No one is judging you," he said calmly.

Kill the boy next door? Sam found himself laughing nervously. "I don't know exactly."

"Did you or do you feel like you might want to harm yourself or others?" Mr. Albertson asked.

"No," he said automatically. He supposed it was the truth. He didn't *feel* like harming anyone, but he was supposed to.

Pastor Joe looked relieved, but Mr. Albertson kept up his level stare as if urging Sam to go on.

"I don't want to harm anyone," he clarified.

"Are there any guns in the house?" Mr. Albertson asked while making more notes.

"No," he again said without a second of thought. Until Aralim had mentioned the gun, there had been one here for years and he'd never known about it. So what was the difference now? It was just like it always had been, here but not.

Mr. Albertson tapped his smooth-shaven chin. "Do you have any pets?"

Sam shook his head. "They cost money, extra food, and that sort of thing. I had a goldfish once. Sianna kept her classroom hamster over one summer when she was in fourth grade."

"A pet can help alleviate anxiety, make you

feel calm, happy," said Mr. Albertson. "Maybe a cat. They typically have less upkeep than a dog." He seemed to catch himself mid-thought. "Oh, but you'll be heading off to college after this year, right?"

"No college for me," said Sam. "I'll have to get a better job though, or a second one. That won't leave any time for a pet."

Pastor Joe leaned forward. "There are scholarships, Samuel. The church even has one. I can look into it for you. I'm sure your mother would like to see you give college a try. It would set a good example for your sister."

The thought of spending another four years struggling with homework made him feel ill. "I'm okay not going, but if you could maybe look into that scholarship for Sianna, I'd appreciate it."

Pastor Joe nodded slowly. He shared a look with Mr. Albertson that Sam didn't quite understand, like they were both saying something to one another without speaking.

"She's smart. Smarter than me, anyway. If one of us should try college, it's her."

He'd be in jail before he'd have a chance to get to college anyway. The news continued to play in the living room. Sam tried to steer the conversation away from himself.

"Do you think they'll catch whoever killed the little girl in Georgetown?" he asked.

The two men glanced at one another. Paster Joe shrugged.

"I heard about that on the news. Tragic story, but the police will take care of it," said Mr. Albertson confidently. "That's nothing you need to worry about."

"I'm not worried. I was just wondering."

Mr. Albertson's raised eyebrow said he didn't believe Sam. "You looked worried and sounded worried. It's good to care about others, Sam, but you don't need to take on caring for everyone." He set his pen down. "I've talked to your principal. She tells me that you might not graduate. The best thing you can do for your family and yourself right now is to focus on you. Focus on your school work."

He held up one hand. "I understand that you need to have a job. It's admirable that you're helping your mother with family expenses. But you need to do what's best for you right now. Just for the next five months. Just long enough to graduate. Maybe cut back on your hours a little, whatever you need to do to make the time you need to complete your assignments."

Momma was harping on him to graduate and so was the principal and his teachers and now Pastor Joe and Mr. Albertson. Graduating would set a good example for Sianna, even if he didn't go to college. He did still have the money he'd earned for watching Henry stashed away. Maybe that would be enough to cover cutting a shift or two a week. But that still meant that he had to do all the school work. Why did senior classes have to be hard? Or maybe they weren't typically but he'd put too many of them off in favor of easy classes until now, when it came down to the wire.

"Maybe," he conceded.

Pastor Joe nodded. "The principal said they have some afterschool resources that she can look into for you that might help you with your assignments."

Why did they care? Any of them? Well, he supposed the principal did because failure on his part would make the school look bad. Momma had probably talked to Pastor Joe about his school problem.

"Would you like to get some help? We don't want to push you into anything you're uncomfortable with," said Pastor Joe.

"I suppose it would help. I haven't picked up the extra shifts I'd dropped when I was watching Henry. So I have three days a week off that I could stay after, I guess."

Mr. Albertson shared another look with Pastor Joe. Pastor Joe appeared reluctant. He cleared his throat.

"I wanted to ask about the angel you saw the other day. Could you tell us more about that?"

"It was just a dream."

"It didn't sound like a dream," said Mr. Albertson.

"It was," he said adamantly.

"Would you like to tell us more about it?" Mr. Albertson asked.

"The dream? I've forgotten most of it now."

"It must have been pretty significant to make you come to church after such a long absence," said Pastor Joe. "I would really like to hear about what you saw in your dream."

Sam considered how much he should say. They watched him like they knew he was keeping things back. Like they thought he was lying. Or maybe that he'd been on drugs, that seemed like everyone's default opinion of him.

"I only remember a little bit. There was an angel, it was super bright. Hard to look at, you know? It didn't have a halo or anything like that. It did have wings though. Huge wings made of white feathers. Or what looked like white feathers. I didn't get close enough to touch them."

"You keep saying 'it'. Did the angel not have features of a male or female?" asked Mr. Albertson as he tapped his pen on his little pad of paper.

"No. It wasn't clearly one or the other. Beautiful, I suppose, but not in any way that was clearly male or female. It said its name was Aralim. Have you heard of that name before?"

"That one doesn't ring a bell. The Bible

mentions many angel names but it doesn't include them all," said Pastor Joe.

"That's all I remember."

"What was the angel wearing?" asked Mr. Albertson.

"A long white shirt and pants? I think?"

"What color skin?"

It sure seemed like Mr. Albertson was on a digging jag. Like Momma got sometimes when she knew he was holding back information. He never liked when Momma started picking after details either.

Not toothpaste white like you, he wanted to say. Pastor Joe would certainly report that back to Momma. Best to be polite. "Does it matter?"

"Just curious," he said.

"Brown like mine, I guess. I wasn't paying much attention to that."

Mr. Albertson scribbled his curiosity onto his pad.

"Did the angel say anything other than its name?" asked Pastor Joe, leaning forward again like he wanted to get closer, maybe see inside Sam's head so he could look at the angel for himself.

"It said I was supposed to do something, but I don't remember what. It was something I didn't want to do."

Mr. Albertson let out a not very subtle or under his breath, "Ah ha."

"That's the terrible thing, you mentioned?" asked Pastor Joe.

"I suppose so. Like I said. I don't remember the details anymore. It was just a lingering feeling when I went to church that day. I didn't go because of the dream. Mrs. Harris invited me. I was being nice."

Pastor Joe sat back and nodded. "I see. Thank you for sharing your dream with us, Samuel. I'll talk to your principal and she'll get the tutoring set up. I'm sure someone will give you the information at school."

"Thank you," he said, meaning more for the fact that he was wrapping up this little intervention than for the help.

"I have a few more questions," Mr. Albertson said, watching Pastor Joe stand.

"I'm sure Samuel has homework to get to, don't you?"

Sam nodded.

"We should be on our way." Pastor Joe didn't wait for Mr. Albertson. He headed right for the entry way closet and opened the door to pull out Mr. Albertson's coat.

The chair scraped across the floor and Mr. Albertson looked none too happy to be herded out the door, but Sam was glad to see them go. He let them out and closed the door behind them, only then realizing he'd never offered them anything to drink. Momma would be gravely offended by his lack of manners. Hopefully she wouldn't quiz Pastor Joe on any of that. Surely, the two of them would report to one another.

With his unwelcome guests gone, Sam opened the box Pastor Joe had brought. He put the food away, thinking about what he could make with each item. The small turkey went into the fridge to start to thaw. He couldn't wait to smell it roasting in the oven. He set the bag of apples on the counter, thinking he might also bake an apple pie. The rest he distributed to the pantry and the fridge. For the next few days, his refrigerator was going to look like Mrs. Harris's. It wouldn't last though. He already missed eating at her house. The kitchen here was mostly the same layout, different color counters, same oak cabinets, similar tile floor. But nothing here sparkled brightly like it did next door. It all seemed tired and faded.

Sam pulled a clean dishcloth out of the drawer by the sink. After locating a bottle of cleaner, he started on the cupboard doors. Next, he moved on to the countertops, the stovetop, and the front of the fridge. When he finished, rinsing out the cloth for the twentieth time, the kitchen looked better, but still not the same. Maybe it was the missing plants in the window sill, the vase of flowers on the island, or fresh fruit in a glass bowl, the little things that made the room feel calmer.

He searched through the cabinets but only found a set of scratched up plastic mixing bowls. That wouldn't do at all. Choosing one of the few chipped china plates that Momma had found at Goodwill, he piled the apples into a pyramid and stood back to admire his work.

"It looks good," said Aralim, suddenly standing next to Sam.

Sam jumped, knocking the apples onto the counter where they rolled off the edge and onto the floor.

"Now they'll be bruised," he grumbled.

"Sorry about that." Aralim picked up the apples before Sam could get to them. He held each one for a second before putting them back into a pyramid on the plate. "Good as new."

"You fixed them?"

"Healed them, yes."

"Thank you." He backed away from the kitchen. "No, I haven't killed anyone today."

"I know. You're not supposed to kill just anyone. And don't think of it that way. You're freeing his soul to be born again."

As if that didn't sound like something a crazy person would say. In fact, he was pretty sure he'd heard a similar rant on one of those crime shows Momma liked to watch when she couldn't sleep.

Sam shot Aralim a glare. "Sure okay, I'll just go get my gun then."

"So, you found the gun."

Could angels look smug? They never did in paintings, but Aralim pulled it off.

"How do I know you didn't plant it there? I would have never even looked for it if you hadn't mentioned it. Isn't that some sort of violation of free will? Interference, at the very least."

"Just doing what I can to help you. Like I said, you could have used your bare hands. You could have pushed him down the stairs instead of letting him fall."

"I didn't let him fall."

The angel shrugged. "You seemed to be having a hard time with that method. Which is understandable given your level of conscience. You'd think that with so many tools at your disposal these days, killing would be easier. Some would say too easy."

"There was less murder when we lowly humans had to use our hands or rocks, huh?"

Aralim nodded. "Less cause for corrections too. You were all wide-spread, plenty of space between tribes and families. Now you're all crammed together, so many of you, and you all want different things. It's hard to keep everything straight."

"There's a straight? How planned out is our future?" Sam eyed the pyramid of apples, thinking about how easily the whole arrangement had crumbled with a single move on his part.

"Even I don't know that. Above my pay-grade, as you humans say." Aralim smirked.

Sam had had enough of the angel's attempts at making light of the situation it had thrown him into. "Why are you here? I've had enough visitors today."

"That's your fault." Aralim surveyed the house from the kitchen. "You could take up the offer for tutoring. Or not. Freewill and all that. Or you can skip it all and do your task. The end result will be the same. Will your struggle to graduate make enough of a difference in the end?"

As if all the air had gone out of the room, Sam gasped and sunk into a chair at the table. "You suck as a motivational angel."

"Not my job. Not a guardian angel either, so don't go looking for me later. I'm just here to make sure the plan remains intact, that the weave doesn't fray."

"A fixer?"

"Something like that."

"Are you saying that I shouldn't bother with graduating?"

"That's not what I said."

Sam let out a groan and rubbed his forehead. "You don't say a whole lot."

"Also not a guidebook."

"Right. Then why don't you just leave me to

my misery."

Aralim rested a hand on Sam's shoulder. A soft warmth seeped through his shirt along with a moment of utter peace.

"I'm sorry it has to be this way, Sam. You are the right choice for this task. You are needed."

"You're wrong. You have to be. God wouldn't ask this of me."

"God doesn't make mistakes."

The peace dissipated, leaving a sense of clarity behind. Sam glared at the angel. "The answer is still no."

13

Sam sat on the couch watching the news with the remaining slice of apple pie. It was his reward after attending the third tutoring session of the week.

The ice cream was long gone, as was the turkey and mashed potatoes. The rolls and beans hadn't made it past Black Friday. He'd left the cranberries to Sianna. She liked them with cream cheese on crackers. The crackers were almost gone too. The fridge was near empty again. The next church box wasn't due for another week. He debated giving Momma grocery money or making her take him with to the store so he could make sure she spent the money on food.

The weather girl talked about rain and the first snow and making sure to get what little sun was going to be available next Wednesday because it would be the last day they'd see it for a while.

He wasn't ready for winter. That meant trying to maneuver his bike through partially plowed roads, bribing Momma to give him rides, or taking twice as long to get to work by walking. The one benefit of living downtown in cop land was that they had a good bus system. Buses didn't go out in the suburbs. People out here had cars. Usually.

If only his father had finished working on the car in the garage. Then Sam would have been more inclined to get his license and would have had a car of his own.

Then again, if his father had finished the car, he probably would have left in it. It had been his prized possession. Sam had toyed with it when he'd turned sixteen, hoping for a quick fix, but the sheer number of parts on the garage floor and all over the work bench and the lack of parts under the hood, had quickly deterred his ambition. As much as he tried to make sense of it all, mechanical stuff just didn't come naturally to him.

The slick male reporter sat at the news desk with a triumphant smile. He announced that the child-killer in Georgetown had been caught. He was going to jail and they would be covering the trial. Did people sit around and watch court proceedings on TV? There was a channel for that. His civics teacher urged them to watch it, but without cable TV, Sam didn't have access to it even if he did want to watch. It sounded about as much fun as watching paint dry.

"How do I look?" Sianna jumped in front of the TV and spun around to show off her short black skirt and low-cut white shirt.

"Date?"

"You think I'm getting dressed up to hang out on the couch with you?" She laughed. "Yes, Rolando will be here in half an hour. So what do you think? Third date worthy or should I change?"

"Is he the baseball guy?"

"Volleyball. Baseball guy didn't make it past date two. He kept looking at every girl who walked down the aisle at the movie theatre."

"Do you just use these dates to get free movies out of these guys?"

She grinned. "No. But that is a perk. Like Momma is gonna give me cash for all the movies I want to see."

"Put a sweater on or something." He pointed the fork at the cleavage peeking over the top of her shirt.

She giggled. "You sound like Momma. More than Momma, even. She'd be borrowing this shirt if I let her."

Sianna was right, but he didn't want to think about Momma dressed like that. It made him all cringy inside.

"You look fine. Just be careful, alright?"

"Always am."

She winked and headed back to the bathroom to likely add more makeup. He didn't understand why girls wore so much of the stuff. It seemed like false advertising.

Sam finished his pie just before the doorbell rang. "Sianna, he's here."

"Can you get it? I'll be right there."

Sam set the plate on the coffee table and went to open the door. Rolando turned out to be a sleek fellow, tall, and well dressed. He looked startled to see Sam.

"Might as well come in. She's in the bathroom." He shook his head.

Rolando snickered. "Thanks."

They'd almost made it back to the couch when Sianna burst from the bathroom to make a grand entrance.

"I'm ready," she announced.

"We get it," said Sam.

Rolando grinned. "You look great."

"Thank you. Shall we?"

Rolando took in her shirt with not near as concealed appreciation as Sam would have liked.

"You'll want a coat. It's almost snowing out there." Sam said, hoping she'd keep the coat on all night.

"Right. One moment." She grabbed what used to be Momma's Sunday coat out of the entry closet. After putting it on, she felt around in the pockets and came out with a victorious whoop. "Check this out!"

Sam peered over to see her holding up a ten-dollar bill. "You know that's stealing, right? And did you ask if you could wear her coat?"

"She hasn't worn it in years, Sam. If she hasn't missed the money by now, she doesn't even remember it's there."

"Go on then," he waved the two of them off. It didn't matter how long it had been since she'd worn that coat, Momma was going to be pissed. At least she wouldn't be mad at him for once.

With the house quiet, the news dragged on. A house fire, a robbery, and a fundraiser that raised a record amount of money for a local non-profit. Why did they always lead with the bad news first? Was this all part of the plan? The tapestry that Aralim talked about? Were other angels guiding people along, nudging them in the correct direction? He'd only heard of crazy people mentioning actually seeing or talking to angels. Those people got off in insanity pleas, got put in institutions. But Aralim hadn't mentioned that as an option for him. Was that a freewill thing?

If he did go through with killing Henry, could he talk his lawyer into pleading insanity? An angel had told him to do it. Surely that made him nuts.

Just thinking about it made him crazy.

Sam turned off the TV and started in on his

homework. He'd thought the tutoring had been helping. His classes made more sense. Some of them did, anyway, but he'd still only got a C on his English essay and a C- on his Algebra test. Was it like Aralim said? Not worth the effort? He hoped it would get better. After spending three days a week after school, it *had* to get better.

Momma's hand on his shoulder brought him awake. Sam sat up groggily to find he had fallen asleep on his civics book. He wiped his eyes and was glad to see he hadn't drooled on the pages. His pencil was still in his hand.

"Why don't you get to bed?" Momma suggested.

"Did you just get home?"

She nodded. "It's after midnight." Momma shooed him toward his room.

"Is Sianna home yet?" he asked.

"You didn't hear her come in?" Momma looked around the kitchen.

"No." Sam got up and slid his homework into his backpack. "She's supposed to be home by eleven, isn't she?"

Momma nodded. She walked over to Sianna's door and opened it. The light was off. She went in but came right back out. "She's not here. She didn't call?"

Sam checked the answering machine. "No messages. I would have heard the phone."

Momma started to look worried. Sam, now

more awake, also noted that her steps weren't all that steady.

"Why don't you sit down," he suggested.

She checked the clock with a frown and then dropped ungraciously into one of the chairs at the table. "I had a few drinks," she said.

Momma did like the bar for date nights. At least she hadn't driven home.

"How was your date?" he asked, trying to pass the time in the hopes that Sianna would walk in the door any minute.

"Oh, just fine. Nothing special. The usual getting-to-know-you stuff."

"Don't you get sick of that? Doing the same date over and over with these guys?"

Momma scowled. "You make it sound like I'm some kind of—"

"I just meant that you go on a lot of first and second dates. I'm curious, what do guys do wrong that you don't want to see them for a third time or longer?"

"You don't like when I have a serious boyfriend," she said sharply.

Sam wracked his mind. "When did I ever say that? We just want you to be happy, Momma."

"I was happy with Nick."

"Nick?" Sam's muscles tightened. "He was no good for you. No good *to* you. How could you want to be with someone who treated you like that?"

"You only notice the bad in people, you know that?" she snapped. "He had a few issues. We all do. But he was sweet sometimes too."

Sam didn't want to hear about whatever Nick did downstairs that Momma thought was sweet.

"Did Sianna say where they were going?" Momma asked after a little while of sulking in silence.

"Movies, I think. Don't know which one."

"Maybe the movie ended later than she thought. Can't just walk out on the end, I suppose."

Sianna was an hour late, but part of him was glad that Momma wasn't going ballistic on her. Drinking calmed her down a bit, but made her moody. She could flip any minute. Then again, he couldn't help but remember the one time he'd stayed to help close at work and got home five minutes after curfew. She'd grounded him for a week. It wasn't fair that she treated Sianna differently. Maybe she got special treatment because they were both girls.

"Do you want a snack?" he asked, thinking maybe if she was busy eating, she would stick with the relatively good mood.

"I couldn't eat another thing. We went to dinner first. Calypso's." She patted her stomach. "All you can eat perch. I ate all I could eat and then some."

It had been so long since he'd gone out to

eat. Calypso's had been his parents favorite place to go as a family. The perch was great. The fries were even better. The ones at work had nothing on Calypso's fries. Now he was hungry. Mrs. Harris always had frozen fries in her freezer.

Filled with optimism, Sam wandered over to the fridge and pulled the freezer door open. An empty ice cube tray, a freezer-burnt package of burger, and a half-empty bag of store-brand chicken nuggets greeted him. He closed the door.

With less enthusiasm, Sam made himself half a peanut butter sandwich and sat back at the table. Momma went downstairs to change out of her usual date night number two dress. By the time she'd returned with her makeup gone, her hair in a scarf, and sweats on, Sianna still wasn't home.

"Twelve-thirty, were is that girl?" Momma huffed and glared at the clock. "I gotta work in the morning."

"And I have school."

"You go on and get to bed. I'll stay up."

Momma put the chairs neatly by the table and adjourned to the couch where she settled in with the book she kept on the coffee table. From what he could remember, she'd been 'reading' it for about a year and a half now. Thankfully it was one Aberdeen had loaned her and not from the library where she would have racked up hefty fees by now.

Sam got ready for bed and slipped beneath

the covers. For once, he wished Aralim would show up so he could ask the angel where Sianna was. A nagging thought in the back of his mind kept telling him to worry. The longer he laid there in the dark, the more his gut agreed.

Thinking back to his conversation with Aralim, when the angel had mentioned not being a guardian angel, it had said *later*. Had the angel meant tonight? Had it known something was going to happen to Sianna?

If you know something about where Sianna is, Sam thought hard at the sky above, *I might be more agreeable to doing my task if you tell me.* He waited in the darkness, hoping to see a burst of light, but the angel didn't answer.

Sam checked the clock. One-thirty. He was sure he hadn't heard the door, but just in case he'd maybe drifted off, he crept out of his room to check.

The lamp was on by the couch but the overhead lights were now off. The front porch light was on. Momma had fallen asleep on the couch. He picked up her book from her lap, moved the dust jacket flap three pages to the new location and set it back on the coffee table.

"Momma?" he said softly.

She jerked awake. "Sianna?"

"She's still not home. I got a bad feeling. Maybe we should go drive around? Look for her?"

"What if she comes home?" Momma asked.

Though he really wanted to go with, if for nothing else than doing something, she had a point. "I'll stay here. Can you go look? Maybe drive the route between here and the movie theatre?"

Momma nodded. "Maybe their car broke down. Darn kids don't know how to fix anything these days. Your father, he could have taken the whole car apart and repaired it by now."

Given that the car in the garage was in a hundred pieces and had been even when his father had lived there, that seemed quite an exaggeration. "Sure, Momma. Just go look."

"I will." She gathered up her purse and keys and slipped back into her heavy winter coat. She gave Sam a quick kiss on the cheek and left.

Sam paced the front door to the front window in the living room to the back door in the laundry room in the hopes that Sianna would try to sneak in knowing she was late. Stars twinkled in the clear night sky. Frost glistened on the grass and the last half of the leaves he hadn't got around to mowing over. It was quarter after two when headlights pulled into the driveway.

He ran to the door to see Momma turning off the car. She sat out there in the dark for so long that his nerves began to tingle. He was just about to reach for his coat when he heard car doors close. Two doors. Relief flooded through him. Must have been car trouble. Everything was fine. He shook his head and let out a deep breath of almost laughter. No need to get all worked up.

He opened the front door.

Momma had her arm around Sianna. Mascara ran down Sianna's cheeks in dark rivulets. Her lipstick was gone. She held Momma' Sunday coat around herself like the big fluffy yellow blanket she used to wrap up in when she was little.

"You found her," Sam said, feeling stupid as soon as the words left his mouth.

Momma nodded. "Sianna, why don't you sleep with me tonight? We can talk if you want to. Or wait til morning."

Sianna sniffed and stared at the floor. She didn't move.

"Are you okay?" Sam asked, reaching out to her.

She flinched and stepped away.

His pulse started to race. "Did Rolando do something?"

Momma gave him a warning glare. The one she used when he was on her last nerve. He hadn't done anything. Not yet, anyway.

"What did he do?" Sam demanded.

"Samuel. Enough. Go to bed. We'll deal with this in the morning."

"No, if something happened, we need to deal with it right now. Haven't you paid attention to any of those crime shows you watch? We call the cops.

We file a report. They do an exam if that's what…"

Momma looked at Sianna. She took her arm and brought her to the couch. "Sit," she said softly.

Sianna sat, still clutching the coat, still keeping her gaze on the floor.

"Do we need to call the police?" Momma asked.

Sianna didn't move.

"We don't need details, honey, but can you nod yes or no?"

Tears rolled down Sianna's cheeks. "It was just a breakup fight, Momma. That's all. We fought and he told me to get out."

"He left you on the side of the street in the middle of the night? What an ass—"

"Samuel, language. Good thing I found you." She patted Sianna's knee.

Sianna shied away from Momma's hand.

"Are you sure?" Sam asked, looking his disheveled sister over and not believing a word of what she said.

She bobbed her head, just once, just a little.

Momma rubbed slow circles on Sianna's back over the coat.

Feeling like he was intruding and that Sianna might say more if he wasn't there, Sam went back to the kitchen. He considered going to his room, but he was too angry to sleep. Clearly the slick little Junior had done something to his sister, something she didn't want to talk about, and his gut told him it had nothing to do with a breakup fight. Sianna had been through plenty of those and had never come home hours late and so out of sorts that she didn't even want Sam to give her a hug.

How dare Rolando come into the house, smiling and laughing, meeting him, and then dare do something uninvited with his sister?

The more he thought about what Sianna had implied with her nod, the angrier he got. Rolando was lucky that Sam didn't know where he lived. After all, he did have a gun.

That thought stopped him dead in his pacing along the counter. If he hadn't known about the gun, he would have never considered using it like this. But he did know. He knew how it felt in his hands and where the bullets were. Why couldn't Aralim asked him to shoot Rolando? He wouldn't have had near as many reservations with that command.

But of course, Aralim wouldn't make it easy. Life wasn't easy, wasn't that the saying? Full of challenges? An adventure. It was feeling like more of a nightmare tonight.

He tried to hear what Momma was saying to Sianna, but they were talking too quietly. Sam forced himself to sit at the table where he could still see the living room clearly, but allowed Sianna and Momma some space.

There was no way he was going to school

tomorrow, not with only a couple hours of sleep. Momma would call in for him. Normally she made him go unless he had a fever or was throwing up, but this was a special circumstance. Kind of like the morning when he'd woken up to find his father had packed up in the night and left without a goodbye.

"I just want to take a shower and go to bed," Sianna shouted. "Just leave me alone."

Stunned, Sam watched his sister hurry through the kitchen and down the hall to the bathroom. Momma followed as far as the kitchen. She looked exhausted.

"That must have been some fight," she said, watching the bathroom door.

"It was more than that, Momma, and you know it."

"She says there wasn't anything else."

"She's lying."

Momma scowled. "Your sister is a good girl. I don't appreciate you implying otherwise."

"I wasn't. I was implying Rolando isn't a good guy."

She shook her head. "You shouldn't always assume the worst. It's late and she's had a rough night."

Sam stood, looking down on his mother and returning her scowl. "Maybe you should assume the worst a little more often." He stormed off to his room.

"You better get what sleep you can. You're not missing school tomorrow. You have tests," she called after him.

He spun around. "You seriously expect me to do well on three tests tomorrow on a few hours of sleep? Just call in for me and I can do a makeup date. That will give me more time to study anyway."

"That's cheating and I'll not have it."

Realizing that she wasn't going to see reason, Sam escaped into his room before he said something that got him kicked out. In the mood Momma was in, she'd probably do it.

Thankfully, no angels waited for him. Sam got under the blankets and stared into the blackness at his ceiling, wondering if he could run into Rolando at school in the morning and what he might do.

14

The next morning, Sam sat outside school as long as he dared, but either he'd missed Rolando arriving or the guy's mother was as forgiving as Momma had been with Sianna and had excused him for the day.

Annoyed, Sam settled into his seat in Algebra. The hour passed with vague recollections of what his tutor had painstakingly explained in minute detail. Even with the test being multiple choice, most of the answer options didn't look right. Why did math have to be like walking in on a foreign language conversation?

By third hour he could barely keep his eyes open. At lunch he spotted Rolando sitting at a table with his volleyball buddies. A burst of anger ignited Sam's energy. He didn't bother going to the lunch line. He stalked straight over to Rolando and shoved him face first into his lunch tray.

A resounding gasp flowed from the guys at the table. A couple of his buddies jumped up from their seats and came at Sam. The lack of sleep made him edgy and beyond reason. On a good day, he would have walked away, he wouldn't have hit Rolando at all. But this wasn't a good day.

Instead, he threw a punch at the volleybro on his left, connecting with his jaw. The guy went spinning away. The volleybro on the right must have had more practice because his fist slammed into Sam's face before Sam got his arm back up.

Everything turned hazy and distant.

When Sam came back to himself, he was standing over three guys who were on the cafeteria floor, bleeding and groaning, one of them was Rolando. A crowd had gathered in a circle around the table. Blood streaked his knuckles.

The school police officer broke through the circle like a red rover champion. Officer Jennings took Sam's arm, twisted it around behind his back, and led him out of the cafeteria to the security office around the corner. He shut the door with a heavy slam.

"Sit."

Sam, now exhausted, took the chair gratefully. He rubbed his throbbing knuckles while Officer Jennings picked up the phone. He pushed a button.

"Nurse? There are three students in the cafeteria in need of medical attention. Yes, thank you." He hung up the phone.

"Now, why don't you tell me what that was all about?"

While Sam searched for coherent words, Officer Jennings clicked on his keyboard. "Your name?"

"Samuel Mason"

More typing. "I haven't had you in here before. Senior year, huh? No afterschool sports. No prior issues." He rubbed his stubbled chin. "Not a fan of volleyball?"

"Rolando, I'm pretty sure he raped my sister last night."

Officer Jennings went still. "I see. And what do you mean by pretty sure? Did your sister file a report with the police?"

"She didn't want to talk about it. But the way she was acting, it sure seemed like that's what happened. She was real upset, came home late... He left her on the side of the street to walk home alone at two in the morning."

"While I agree, leaving anyone alone on the street side at two in the morning wouldn't be my favorite person either, I can't condone your fighting in school. If your sister isn't going to file a report, then there's nothing I can do on your other accusation either. With no proof, it's hard to make those charges stick."

"I know. I watched the movies in health class,"

Sam grumbled

"Then I'm sure you've read the school policy on fighting as well."

Officer Jennings sighed and leaned back in his chair. "If your sister is willing, we do have resources to help her here, counseling and that sort of thing. She can set up an appointment anytime." He passed Sam a half sheet of paper with the school logo on the top and a list of names and contact information. "There are community resources on the back side if she would rather talk to someone outside of school."

"Thanks."

"As to you, the principal has issued a suspension."

"What about Rolando? Is Sianna supposed to come back to school with him like nothing happened? I'm pretty sure they have a few classes together."

Officer Jennings put his elbows on his desk and tapped his fingers together. "Again, we don't have any proof or official statements to say that anything did happen last night between Rolando and Sianna. So yes, school will continue as usual. She can, however, ask to switch her schedule around if or when she talks with one of the school counselors."

That didn't seem fair. Sianna hadn't done anything wrong, but she was the one who had to rearrange her schedule? Sam was about to voice his feelings on the matter when Officer Jennings started typing on his computer. His printer spat out a paper that he slid across the desk to Sam.

"You'll need to fill that out and sign it. I'll give you a few minutes, and then, when you're finished, your suspension will go into effect and I will escort you off of the school grounds. You will not go near Rolando again or further action will be taken against you."

"Yes, sir."

"Good. You seem like a good kid, Samuel. Let's keep this to an isolated incident, alright?"

Sam nodded.

Officer Jennings handed him a pen and then walked out of the office. From the sound of the conversation outside, he wasn't far from the closed door. Sam glanced over the form. He picked up the pen and quickly wrote down why he'd attacked Rolando and his friends.

His knuckles hurt, but he didn't mind in the least. All he kept thinking about was pounding Rolando's taco-sauce-splattered face. Feeling satisfied, he sat back and waited for Officer Jennings to come back in.

Officer Jennings looked over what Sam had written and set the paper on his desk. "A copy will be mailed home and also kept in your school record. A parent will need to sign and return the mailed form before you can return to school. Do you understand?"

Sam nodded. Momma wasn't going to be happy about that, but the fight was justified. She'd understand. It wasn't like he went around starting fights. Ever. Until today.

"Alright then. Do you need to visit your locker or call for a ride?"

"My backpack and coat are in my locker. I rode my bike."

"Good deal."

Officer Jennings stood, opened the door, and followed him to his locker.

Sam filled his backpack with all of his books, figuring he might as well use his three days off productively and then lugged the heavy load onto his shoulder. It wasn't often he had to take every book home.

The fifth hour bell rang. People poured out of classrooms and past Sam. They whispered as he walked by. Faces hovered behind locker doors and others turned away as people motioned after him.

"Eyes forward," Officer Jennings said quietly. "Outside."

Sam nodded, making his way to the front door slowly. He wanted to hear what people were saying, but all he could pick up were hushed words: *rape, punched him hard, face meets taco, three on one*. At least he'd accused Rolando of rape at some point in his fighting rage. He hoped word of that spread. That it spread just as much as the rumors of his sister being a slut. She wasn't.

Once they were outside, Officer Jennings stood back while Sam unlocked his bike and slipped his backpack strap over his other shoulder. With the heavy weight evenly distributed, he got onto his bike.

"Make sure your parent signs the form."

"I will."

"When you get home, put some ice on your hands. That will help."

"Thanks."

Officer Jennings nodded and waved him off.

Banished from school, Sam took his time getting home. He had to work soon anyway. Maybe if he took his time, he could arrive home as usual and then save the whole suspension thing for tomorrow's problem with Momma. She had her hands full with Sianna anyway. He was doing her favor.

He managed to get home close enough to his normal time that Momma didn't notice he was a few minutes early. She sat on the couch, staring at the TV. It wasn't even on.

"Hi Momma."

"How was your day?" she asked, slowly turning toward him. Dark circles lined her dull eyes.

"Not very good. How's Sianna?"

"Hasn't come out of her room. She slept with me a little. I think. You need to give her some space, okay? She's not thinking too favorably of men right now."

"I will."

"Good boy. You better get yourself something to eat and work on that homework before you head out to flip the burgers."

"Actually, I've been on drive-thru lately. It's nice."

"That's good," she said absently.

"Momma, why don't you take a nap? I'll let you know when I have to leave. Get a little rest."

"Thank you, Sam. I just might do that." She stood up as if her body didn't need to give that suggestion any thought. A minute later she was headed down the stairs on autopilot.

Sam made a peanut butter sandwich and poured a glass of water. Sitting down at the table, he set into his after-school feast.

Sianna slipped out of her room. She cast a hesitant glance his way.

"Have a seat. I'll make you one."

She nodded and came over to sit silently at the table.

He got busy in the kitchen, making her a sandwich and then sliding a plate and glass in front of Sianna.

"I beat the snot out of Rolando today," he said offhandedly.

She paused mid bite to look at him, actually look, for the first time since she'd come home.

"And two of his friends."

She almost smiled.

"Officer Jennings gave me a paper for you. If you want to talk to anyone about, you know, whatever happened."

"You got sent to the campus police officer?" she whispered.

"He pulled me out of the fight. Though the other guys were on the ground, so does that count as pulling me out?" He felt pretty good about his accomplishment in the cafeteria boxing ring.

"You didn't."

He nodded.

"You don't get into fights. Ever."

"I do for you."

Tears welled in her eyes. "Thank you."

"I wish I could do more."

"Me too. I don't think I can go back there," she said quietly.

"To school? Officer Jennings said if you talk to a counselor, they could make any necessary schedule adjustments."

"But he's there," she whispered.

"So it wasn't just a fight."

Sianna bowed her head. "I don't want to talk

about it."

"Alright, but if you want to with someone else..." Sam pulled out the half sheet of paper and set it by Sianna's hand.

Sianna nodded slowly. "More than seeing him, God only knows what he's told everyone else by now."

"I can tell you what I said to his face and what people were saying about that. It wasn't in his favor, you can be sure."

She finally did smile. "Have I told you lately that you're my favorite brother?"

"Not lately." He chuckled.

Sianna's smile vanished and her gaze dropped to her hands on the table. "I know what people said about me, that they called me a slut, but I swear I didn't do anything but a little fooling around before. You know how guys exaggerate to impress each other."

"I've heard, yeah. We don't all do that."

"I know, Mr. Loner. But the rest of them thrive off each other, like a pack of bragging wolves."

"Quite accurate."

"It didn't bother me before because I knew it was all lies. But now..." she shook her head. "I don't think I can face any of them. I can't go back there."

"Maybe Momma will let you do online school?"

"On our ancient computer?"

Sam did a quick count of the babysitting funds

he had left and knew he fell far short of what he'd need to buy a better computer. "Maybe we could borrow one from the school?"

She picked up the paper. "I suppose I could ask a counselor about that."

Glad she was willing to talk to someone about something, Sam offered her an encouraging smile.

Sianna stood. "I think I'm going to take another shower." She grabbed the paper and headed to her bedroom in slow motion, her feet dragging. While she'd at least had a little spark of herself for a few minutes, it had drained out quickly. That was all Rolando's fault.

Sam changed into his uniform and said goodbye to Sianna through the bathroom door before taking his bike to work. Grateful he'd put off the inevitable confrontation with Momma for a few hours, he pedaled to his job with a single-minded focus.

His manager made a point of looking right at Sam's reddened knuckles and asked him twice that night if he was okay. Sam said he was. He was, compared to Sianna.

He didn't say much of anything to anyone other than to take orders from customers and make change. If he took too long between tasks, his mind began to replay the fight with Rolando. He began to remember what he'd said. What he'd threatened, and it made him break out into a sweat.

He'd never been mad like that before.

Was that what it was like for some of the men his mother dated? Was he going to end up like them? Their ugly side mostly came out when they were drinking. He'd never touched a drop of alcohol for that very reason. But maybe everyone had ugly inside, just sitting there coiled up and seething, waiting for an excuse to lash out.

When his shift was over, he started for home. The autumn evening had fallen fast and hard. The streetlights seemed to barely penetrate the heavy blackness. The chill of the afternoon air had turned to freezing temperatures, lending its touch to what tried to be rain, but was instead sleet being driven sideways by a blustery wind that knocked him around on the road. Sam pulled his hood tighter and wished he'd worn gloves. Though the cold and wet did make his aching hands numb.

By the time he reached home, he couldn't feel his fingers at all. They had cramped around the handlebar of the bicycle. Painfully, he unclenched his hands and set the bike against the garage before dashing inside. Momma sat on the couch with her book in her hands.

"Hi, Momma." Sam shook out his coat on the big rug by the door. Ice and snow fell to the floor. His entire coat was soaked and dripping.

"Better go put that in the sink in the laundry room. Nasty weather out there."

She could have given him a ride. She knew he was working and that he was closing. He always kept his schedule on the fridge.

"I know. A ride would have been nice." His teeth were chattering and his ears were starting to burn now that he was inside.

"Can't say as I was feeling very charitable after the call from the principle this afternoon."

So she was mad. But to make him bike home in the freezing rain? That seemed like cruel and unusual punishment. He wasn't above pouring on a little guilt given how miserable he was. "Let's hope I don't get sick from being out in the cold."

"Good thing you have three days at home to recover if you do," she said without mercy and still not looking up from her book.

"Come on, Momma. He deserved it."

"That might be, but I raised you better than that."

Freezing and aggravated to the point where he was about to regret anything else he said, Sam headed for his room without another word.

15

Sam heard the doorbell. No one was supposed to be home and he wasn't dressed yet so he ignored it. The firm knock that followed a moment later made him curious. Either this was a really determined door-to-door salesman or something important. What if it was Mrs. Harris or one of the other neighbors? Sam threw on a sweatshirt, pulled up his pajama pants, and went over to peek out the front window.

A police officer stood on the doorstep. He lifted his finger to the doorbell again.

Sam pulled the door open. "Can I help you?"

"Is your mother home?"

"She's at work. Did the school contact you about my sister filing charges against Rolando?"

The officer, a thick-waisted, middle-aged white man with a bushy grey-flecked mustache stared him down. "No. I'm here about the threats you made against Rolando Ortega yesterday at school. He's filed a report against you. And he has witnesses to back him up. You made death threats?"

"I was really mad. I didn't mean them though. I'd never hurt anyone like that."

The officer didn't ease up. "You're eighteen, correct?"

Sam nodded.

"This is a warrant." He held up a paper. "I'm going to need to speak with your parent, as the owner of the house. I have her number," he said before Sam could offer to call her. "Please get your ID. I'll need to verify that too."

Sam left the door open, closing it in the officer's face seemed rude, while he dashed to his room to grab his school ID. When he returned, the officer was on his phone. Sam could hear his mother's voice on the other end.

"Yes, of course, you have my permission to search the house. We don't own any guns, but if you find one, you get it out of there. Put Sam on a minute, would you?"

Uninvited, Sam held out his hand. Momma was using her polite but loud voice, which meant she was super pissed, but holding it all in. "Hello, Momma."

"What did you do, Samuel? Death threats?" He could see her jaw working and feel her glare just by her tone.

"I didn't mean anything by it. I swear. It's just

something you do in a fight, you know?"

"I don't fight people, so no, I do not know. We're discussing this later. Cooperate. I mean it. Do not give those officers any reason to look at you twice. Best behavior. I mean it."

"Yes, Momma." He handed the phone back to the officer along with his ID.

After the officer finished on the phone and handed the ID back. He motioned to someone behind him. "We're cleared to do the search."

Officer Jennings, who had escorted him off the school grounds, came in. "Hi Sam. The school takes these threats very seriously and since Rolando and his parents came to us, we are required to look into it. Do you have any guns in the house?"

Sam shook his head.

"Are you sure?" asked the older officer. "We show a handgun registered to a Tyrell Mason at this address."

"No, sir. He walked out on us years ago. Took all his stuff with him."

The officer frowned but nodded. "Is your sister here?"

"In her room. She's mostly been in there since... I don't know if she's even awake yet."

"It's eleven," said Officer Jennings.

Sam shrugged. Everyone knew that teenagers slept in, didn't they?

"Here's what's going to happen," explained the

school officer. "You need to stay at the table over there," he pointed to the kitchen. "We're going to go through the house. We'll be careful, but we do have your mother's permission to do a search."

"Sure. Can I have breakfast while you do it?"

The older officer rolled his eyes. "Sure." He walked away, muttering about the last time he'd had eight solid hours of sleep. "I'll check the basement," he called out from the stairs.

Officer Jennings looked around the main floor, keeping an eye on Sam as he worked. The basement hallway light flipped on a moment later. He popped in and out of rooms, keeping tabs on Sam every few minutes. Sam munched on his cereal, watching the live cop show taking place in his house.

When the two of them concluded their search, they met up at the kitchen table. "Could you to wake your sister? Hers is the only room we haven't searched," asked the school officer.

He would have rather that they didn't search Sianna's room at all, but he knew that would look suspicious.

"Sure. One moment." Sam knocked on her door until he heard her stirring around inside. "Sianna, the police are here. They need to look in your room."

Her door popped open. "Police? Look in my room for what?"

"A gun."

Her mouth dropped open. "What?"

"It will only take a moment, Ms. Mason."

"Momma doesn't allow guns in the house." Sianna shook her head, but gestured into her room. "But if you must, go ahead."

"Thank you, Ms. Mason."

"Why do they think we have a gun in the house?" Sianna whispered to Sam.

"I guess I threatened to shoot Rolando during our fight."

She gasped. "You guess?"

"I don't really remember a whole lot of what I said or did. It all just kind of happened."

"That was a stupid thing to do," she said, wrapping her arms around herself. She wore the same pink sweatpants and t-shirt she'd had on the day before. Her thick black curls sprang from what might have been a ponytail yesterday.

"I didn't mean it. You know I wouldn't hurt anyone like that."

"I didn't think you'd actually punch anyone either." She pointed to his swollen knuckles.

"That's different. Definitely not a death threat."

She paled. "I didn't think of that. Sam, what if they ban you from school? Like for good? With all those school shootings everywhere, they have to take this stuff seriously."

"Let's hope not." His skin crawled. Why hadn't

he kept his mouth shut and his temper in check? Why had he given into rage this one time? Sam glanced at his sister. Oh yeah, that's why.

"I'm serious, Sam. You could be in big trouble."

"I already am. Or haven't you noticed that I was suspended for three days?"

"Momma told me. She's not happy."

"I picked up on that."

The officers reemerged from Sianna's room.

"All clear. We'll report our findings to the school," said the school officer.

"And I'm going to ask you to stay away from Rolando Ortega. Once. Do you understand me, Mr. Mason?"

"Yes, sir."

Sam let the officers out and went back to sit at the table, deflated. The fight didn't seem quite as worthwhile as it had at the time. Any relief he'd felt with causing Rolando pain to make up for whatever he'd done to Sianna, fled his mind. Momma was going to be livid once she got home, considering she now knew of his threats and that cops had searched the house. He glanced around, verifying that they'd been respectful of their belongings. Everything seemed relatively in place, maybe shuffled around a little, but not thrown about like cops often did on TV.

With Momma's impending arrival looming in his mind, Sam spent the day cleaning his room and vacuuming the rest of the house. When he heard Momma put her purse and keys on the table in the entryway, his heart plummeted to his feet. Frozen in place, he stayed in the safety of his room.

"You better get out here Samuel, because if I have to hunt you down, you're going to be even more sorry."

Sam crept out of his room, still in the pajama bottoms and t-shirt, the uniform of a kid home from school. "Hi Momma."

"Don't 'Hi Momma' me, Samuel. Do you realize what you've done?"

"I'm sorry," he said, hoping to sidetrack her tirade.

"At least they didn't find any guns," she said, her voice rising and words hurling out faster. "To back up the threat you made to shoot Rolando Ortega. You made death threats? My son made death threats? Who are you? What were you thinking?"

"I wasn't, Momma. I'm sorry."

"The school has agreed to let you continue classes online, but you are not allowed back on school grounds. And if you do, if you so much as go near that boy, or make any other threats to any student, you will be expelled. Expelled, Samuel. Do you know what that means?"

"Yes, Momma."

"How could you do this?" She let out a sob,

tears welling in her eyes. "After all you've worked so hard for. My good boy, nearly getting expelled in his last semester before graduation."

"I'm sorry. I didn't mean to do any of this."

"Seems your father is alive in you after all." She turned away.

She rarely spoke of his father and when she did, it wasn't good. Now she was lumping him in with his negligent parent? That hardly seemed fair. Was she throwing him in with Rolando too? Was he bad just because he was male or was it something more?

Before he could ask, she said over her shoulder, "I've asked the school to allow Sianna to take online classes too. They're providing laptops for both of you. I'll pick them up tomorrow on my way to work. And return the forms that came in the mail today about your suspension and the report you neglected to give me to sign when you got kicked out." She shook her head. "Quite a mess you've managed to make. Your father was good at that too. Guess you come by it naturally."

He watched, stunned by her insult, as she walked down the stairs. Hoping to make amends, he asked, "What would you like for dinner, Momma?"

"I'm not hungry and I don't want to look at you right now. Make sure your sister eats something." She turned out the lights at the bottom of the stairs and closed her bedroom door a moment later.

Sam glanced at Sianna's closed door and then went to his room. He sat on his bed staring at Henry's Squidman. It seemed so long ago that he'd been happy, full, on the way to something good with extra cash in his pocket. Now he was on the verge of losing everything. He pulled aside the blanket from his window and stared at the house next door. Henry's light was on as was the one in the kitchen. Mrs. Harris was no doubt making something for dinner and good smells were swirling through the house. His stomach rumbled.

The fact that he'd not see anyone at school again started to sink in. Not his teachers that had been trying to help him, not the two tutors he'd been meeting with after school. Would the few classmates he loosely called friends miss him? Would they even notice that he was gone? Rumors had to be flying through the school by now, everything blown out of proportion and Rolando was probably still there to offer a defense, to be a victim of the threats Sam had thrown out in his tirade.

He rubbed his knuckles. Had his father gotten into fights too? Momma sure made it sound like he had, but Sam didn't remember hearing anything about that when he was younger. Then again, was that something parents talked about to their kids? There were plenty of nights that he remembered

Momma being home alone. She'd always had some excuse why his father wasn't there when he and Sianna wanted to tell him goodnight. They hadn't seemed suspicious then, but now he began to wonder. Had he been cheating on Momma? Had he been out drinking? A host of unsavory possibilities ran through his mind.

Whoever his father had been outside of the house, Sam wasn't him. He wouldn't be. He wouldn't disappoint Momma again.

<h1 style="text-align:center">16</h1>

Online school was far worse than in person. Sam sat on one side of the table, his loaner laptop in front of him, the English lecture on allegory droning through his earbuds. None of it made sense. The words all slurred together, sliding off his brain like a greased cookie sheet.

His stomach demanded cookies. Pastor Joe's recent food box delivery hadn't included any of those, but he had apologized for Mr. Albertson's overzealous interogation. That made up for the lack of sweets.

Sianna sat across from him, staring at her laptop. It had been three weeks since Rolando had left her by the side of the road but she still seemed hollow, fragile, shattered like grandma's vase. Nothing he did or said brought more than a momentary spark of herself to the surface.

"Did you ever contact the school counselor?" he asked, hoping he wasn't coming off like Momma.

She shook her head. "Since we're doing online school, I didn't need to."

"But what about…"

"No," she said curtly.

Sam sighed, missing his sister like she had been before the night with Rolando. She used to love dressing for school, creating a new outfit every day from her Goodwill finds. Now she wore a rotation of the same three sweatshirts and pajama pants. She hadn't put on makeup since her date with Rolando. And she was barely eating, claiming she didn't feel well.

Though he'd been going to work, the snow was falling more often and heavier, making it much harder to get there or home. Momma hadn't been offering to give him a ride like she used to. She wasn't talking to him when she was around. Not that she was home much.

"Do you think she hates us?" Sianna asked, breaking the silence that had settled over them.

"You? No. Me, maybe."

She shrugged. "She barely says anything to me. And she has this look, like she's always disappointed. Like I did something wrong."

"You didn't. Don't mind her. She's…I don't even know." Sam paused his lecture and closed his laptop. "She hasn't even mentioned Christmas and it's in four days. Do you want to take a break and decorate? We could surprise her."

"I'm not feeling much like doing Christmas this year. Sorry, Sam, I haven't even made anything. I don't have any gifts to give. That would make for a pretty sucky Christmas."

"I'm sure Momma has done some shopping. She always does."

"When? She hurries home from work to make sure we're doing our assignments. Then she's either upstairs venting to Aberdeen or out for dinner with whatever his name is this week. I doubt she's shopping with him."

"We'll figure something out. It's Christmas."

"Don't waste your money, Sam. You need it."

He didn't like her ominous tone. "What do you mean?"

"She's going to kick you out as soon as school is done. You're eighteen." She rubbed her hands over her gaunt face and through her uncombed hair. "She hasn't told you yet, but she's talked to me about it. I keep telling her to tell you. A person needs some warning for something like that."

"No kidding." He'd known Momma wasn't happy with him, but to kick him out? That seemed extreme. Or maybe she'd been planning this all along. She'd always implied he should leave for college. Now that it was clear he wasn't doing that, she apparently wanted him to just leave.

"How is she going to pay the bills on her own?"

"She said she'd take a part time night job. I

offered, but she wants me to concentrate on school. She's sold on one of us going to college, but Sam, I don't think I can."

"Why not? You've got good grades. Your teachers like you. I'm sure you'll qualify for a bunch of scholarships."

Sianna closed her eyes and bowed her head. "I'm pregnant."

Sam hadn't given Aralim much thought over the past month, but now the angel's words came crashing in around him. "How?"

She gave him a deadpan stare.

He didn't know if he really wanted confirmation of what had happened that she didn't want to talk about, but the questions were out before he could take them back. "Who? When? Rolando?"

Sianna nodded, the same heart-crushing tiny nod that she had the night Momma had found her walking home.

"But that was only a few weeks ago. You can't tell that fast, can you?"

"I had Momma drop me off at Maria's the other night. A girls' night, you know? She was more than happy to see me get out of the house."

He must have been at work. He hadn't known she'd been gone.

"Maria got a test for me. They work as soon as two weeks. It was positive."

"They can be wrong," he said quickly.

"I'm pretty sure that it's not."

The rotten angel had known. It had seen the weave or whatever it had called it. It knew exactly what Rolando was going to do to Sianna and it hadn't said anything, done anything. When he saw Aralim next he was going to have a lot to say to the angel. Or Demon. Or whatever it was.

Anger boiled up inside him followed quickly by panic. "Momma doesn't know?"

Sianna shook her head. "Not yet, but she'll figure it out eventually."

She was only sixteen. How was she going to graduate with a baby to take care of? And how were they going to afford taking care of a baby, especially if Momma made him leave.

"You have to tell her. If she knows, she'll let me stay. You'll both need my help here."

"Maybe." Sianna closed her laptop. "I'm going to take a nap."

Sam reluctantly returned to his lecture. It was hours later when he looked up from his laptop to find that Momma had come home. She hung up her coat and walked into the kitchen with the pinched look she so often wore now.

"I need to talk to you." She dropped into the chair across from him with Sianna's closed laptop in front of her.

Sam considered confronting her with the

knowledge that she was going to kick him out, but in the hopes that this was something different, he stayed quiet.

"I've been monitoring your progress at school. Both of you. Your principal suggested I pay more attention to your student accounts. She got me signed up with parent access. I can log in at work for that."

For the first time in his life, she was paying attention to his schoolwork now? Not the eleven years of missed parent teacher conferences? Not the award ceremonies in secondary school? Not any of the school carnivals he'd wanted to attend in elementary school. The anger he'd felt earlier exploded so fast the he didn't have time to catch it.

"Now you care?"

"You're failing, Samuel. Unless you can pull off a miracle, there's no way you'll graduate with your class."

Miracles were hardly his thing, according to Aralim.

"It doesn't really matter, does it? Since I can't be with my class. The stupid diploma is just a piece of paper. I can get that in the mail. I'll take summer classes."

"And who is paying for those?"

Her face said it wasn't going to be her. "Me, I suppose."

"You might as well pick up all the hours that

you can, or get a better paying job, because," she drew herself up and looked straight at him, "when graduation day comes, I want you out, whether you get your diploma or not. That's your choice. I've done all I can for you. This mess you're in, that is your doing. All you. Only you can pull yourself out. You're an adult now, or close enough to one, you need to figure it out."

"I'm helping you here. How can you keep up with the bills on your own?"

"I'm going to sell the house, get something smaller. Sianna will be off to college in a couple years. The two of us will manage until then."

"And how are you going to pay for her to go to college?"

"She'll get scholarships, take a couple loans, she'll figure it out. She's a smart girl."

"Maybe she doesn't want to go." That was easier to say than exposing Sianna's secret.

"Don't be stupid. Of course, she's going to go. Someone in this family has to make something good of themselves."

"Maybe we're good just as we are."

She laughed. "Yeah, right."

Sam stood, his teeth grinding together. He'd never been this mad at Momma before. "What about Christmas?"

"It hardly seems like a year for celebration. We all need to save our money. How about we just call it good with a nice dinner from whatever Pastor Joe brings by?"

"Sure," he bit out, not believing she would skip Christmas. In all his life, he'd never considered that was even an option. Everyone celebrated Christmas, or whatever other holiday they called it. Even with as little as they'd had, they'd always exchanged gifts, put up the ragged little plastic tree and the box of dollar store ornaments. They hung up stockings, the ones they'd made when his father had been around, with their hand prints painted on the front and their names written in his father's handwriting. One of the few things they had of him. And now she wanted to skip it all?

"You're both getting too old for all of that stuff anyway. Santa is a thing of the past. Let's face reality this year, Sam."

Not caring much for reality just then, he turned and stormed off to his room. The blinking holiday lights on the Harris' house made him even more angry. He grabbed the blanket curtain and tucked the edges against the window trim, blocking out the Christmas tree in the living room window with its bright white lights and the big red and white Be Merry wooden sign on their porch. The lights outside shone in around the edges of the blanket, reminding him of Aralim's light. Reminding him of what he was supposed to do.

17

Aralim chose Christmas Eve to burst into Sam's bedroom, all blinding light and annoyance. "I've told you there's an expiration date on this agreement, right?"

"You could have told me to not let Sianna go on her date last time I saw you. But you didn't. You didn't bother. Do you even care what happened to her or what it has done to her?"

"I did tell you that she would get pregnant."

"You didn't mention that it would be against her will."

"And we're back to that again, aren't we?" Aralim shook its head slowly. "She didn't have to go on the date. She didn't have to go out with *him* or say what she did. There were options, better ones. Free will landed her in this particular situation."

Sam picked up the lamp that didn't work anyway and threw it at the angel. The dead light bulb flickered and lit as it arced through the air, the unplugged cord dangling loosely behind.

Before it hit Aralim, giant white feathered wings snapped around Sam and the lamp, containing him, and shutting out the light. He couldn't feel Aralim exactly, only the wings. His mind told him that he should be pressed tight against the angel because he couldn't move. Instead, he felt held, but not directly restrained, like the wings had formed a protective cocoon around him. As if time suddenly resumed, the lamp fell to the floor at his feet.

The sensation of floating, of everything troubling him falling away, hit Sam like the warmest blanket, comforting, safe. He breathed deep. If this was at all what heaven felt like, he desperately wanted to go there.

"Like this, but more," whispered Aralim. "Do your task. You'll be there soon."

The reality of the task brought Sam back to his body, back in the bedroom overlooking Henry's house, the boy he was supposed to kill.

Henry's Squidman fell off the bedside table, landing face first on the floor. Tears welled in Sam's eyes.

"I don't want to."

"And that's why you'll get the deal. Only after you complete your task."

Having felt what he had, experienced it himself, Sam nodded. Not that he was any more inclined to hurt Henry, but he really wanted to feel that again, to be able to feel it without a horrible task hanging over his head.

"Progress then. You have the gun. You have access to the boy. Time is ticking, Samuel. Pull the trigger." Aralim vanished.

The air in the room felt charged, electric. Sam shivered. Aralim might be gone from sight, but it sure felt like he was still there, lurking, spying. Watching.

Sam picked up the lamp and set it back on the table. He stood at the window, peeking through the edge of the blanket, staring at the blinking lights next door, watching the shadows dance in Henry's room upstairs. He probably had his own decorated Christmas tree in his room. There was no way Sam was going to complete his task before Christmas. He wouldn't take that from Mrs. Harris. She would have her son and he would have his magical Christmas morning, his mountain of presents and wrapping paper.

Sam walked out of his bedroom and into the living room devoid of a single indication of the holiday season. He sat at the table and opened his laptop. For the next several hours he stared at the screen and his fingers tapped the keys but he was only half aware of what he was seeing or doing. All he really wanted was to crawl back into the feeling Aralim had shown him, the quiet peace of everything being as it should.

Nothing here was as it should be. Not how he wanted it to be.

Giving up on his school work for the day, he headed into the kitchen to bake a pie. If Momma didn't want anything but a nice dinner, he would make sure they had at least that. The box Pastor Joe had brought by earlier in the week had less than they'd received in years past but it was enough to get by on. He'd taken his bike to the supermarket to get a few things the box had been lacking.

The rest of the afternoon passed with making food for the next day, including a special overnight French toast recipe he'd found online. He didn't mind peanut butter sandwiches and leftover fast food, but on Christmas, they'd eat like they belonged in this neighborhood.

Sianna's door remained closed. She only came out of her room to eat for the most part. He missed her smiles and her teasing. When Momma got home from work, she said hello, but that was about it. He tried to ask about her day, but she didn't have much to say before she ducked out of the kitchen and went to talk to Sianna. Sam went into his room, changed for work and then bundled up for the bike ride.

No longer having to deal with actually going to school or his tutoring sessions, he hadn't been late in weeks. He was even ten minutes early today.

A couple of the guys were outside taking a break when he got there.

"Hey Sam," said Mike who was handing Arik something small.

Arik looked nervous.

"Don't worry. Sam's cool. Right, Sam?"

"Sure." Sam ignored them and locked up his bike.

"You know what, being Christmas and all, I'm in the giving spirit." Mike slapped a little clear plastic bag with four round white pills inside into Sam's hand. "Free sample. You like those, I'll have more next week. Sixty bucks."

Sam was about to hand the bag back but Arik was watching and so was Mike. Like really watching. Like they both wanted to confirm that he was in fact 'cool'. He knew some of the guys at work took pills. He even knew Mike was a dealer, but he'd never said anything to anyone about it. He'd been asked if he was interested, both in school and by co-workers but he'd politely declined. No one had ever just handed him anything before. If Momma knew he had drugs in his hand she'd flip a lid for sure.

He stared at the bag and the four pills inside it. Then again, Momma barely spoke to him anymore. She was actually skipping Christmas just to spite him. It wasn't like she hadn't asked him if he was on drugs before. Like anytime he did something she felt he hadn't thought through or when he failed a test. If she was so sure he was already doing this stuff, why was he so hung up on not doing it?

Sam slid the bag into his pants pocket. "Thanks, man. Merry Christmas."

Mike chuckled. Arik relaxed and lit a cigarette.

He lingered there for an awkward moment but eager to get warm and not sure what else to say, Sam went inside. He clocked in with a few minutes to spare.

On Christmas morning, Sam woke up early to put the French toast in the oven. No one else was up. No Christmas tree, no lights, not a single decoration. The only indication that a holiday should be happening were the three Christmas cards stuck to the refrigerator: one from Alberdeen, one from Momma's boss, and one from her insurance agent.

He glanced into the living room at the corner where the ragged tree usually stood, hoping that perhaps Momma had snuck a couple presents in after all, but there really was nothing there. He wasn't about to let Christmas pass with nothing, not if this was going to be his last one with his family.

While breakfast finished baking, he got

dressed and pulled out the two wrapped packages he'd spent most of his babysitting money on. He brought them out to the table and then went downstairs to knock on Momma's bedroom door before coming back up to Sianna's.

Sianna came out, robe on and still half asleep. She sat at the table and pondered the small wrapped box on her plate. "What's this? I thought we weren't doing Christmas?"

"No, Momma said *she* wasn't doing Christmas. That's for you."

"But I didn't get you anything." She rubbed her face, looking slightly more awake. "What smells so good?"

Sam gestured for her to get her present off her plate so he could scoop out a couple slices of French toast for her.

She took a bite. "This is fantastic." Sianna shoved more into her mouth.

Sam watched the stairs but didn't see Momma. She'd mumbled something when he'd knocked on her door so he knew she'd heard him. Maybe she was getting dressed. He sat down and ate a few bites while he waited.

"Momma," he yelled, "Come eat."

They were both nearly finished when she came up and planted herself at the table. She gave the box on her plate a narrow-eyed stare. "What's this?"

Sam grinned. "Open it and find out."

Sianna, needing no further urging, tore the paper off her box. She squealed. "You got me a phone?"

"I did. If you ever need a ride home, you can call. You'll never be alone on the roadside again."

She jumped up from the table and hugged him. "Thank you. I mean it," she whispered in his ear.

He held his sister, enjoying having her exuberant self back, even if only for a moment.

"Where'd you get the money for that?" Momma asked.

"I have a job."

He'd expected her to be happy, maybe appreciate that he'd done something nice for his sister. He'd given her something that she needed, something that would have possibly prevented what had happened between her and Rolando. If she'd known she could have gotten a ride home earlier, maybe she wouldn't have stayed with him after the movie. Maybe she would have dared to get out of the car and start walking before he'd done what he'd done.

Momma shook her head. "I told you to save that money. You're going to need it." She heaved a sigh and then pulled the paper off to reveal a plain brown box. Pulling the tape off the top, she peeked inside. With another sigh, she pulled out the gift.

"It's not the same as Grandma's vase, but it's as close as I could find. The table looked so empty without it."

"That's sweet of you Sam, but I mean it. You take that back to wherever you got it and save your money." She put the vase back in the box. "I'm serious, and you better be too. Sianna, give him the phone."

Sianna clutched her new phone to her chest.

"No. That's hers," Sam said adamantly. "You will not take that away from her. You don't want to do a tree or decorations or whatever else, fine. But we're going to enjoy Christmas. So have some breakfast. I have everything in the fridge for lunch later.

Momma groaned. "How much did you waste on food, Samuel?"

How could she not appreciate what he was trying to do? That he'd made food? She normally was happy about that. She liked when he did nice things for Sianna. For her too.

He'd been doing his schoolwork. His grades had gone back into at least D territory instead of failing. He had been putting money away. Why couldn't she just be happy for one flipping day?

"I didn't waste anything. Most of the food came from the church box."

"Most is not all." She shook her head. "You've got to start thinking about how you're going to support yourself. I promise you; you won't be eating fancy French toast when you're on your own. Pennies, every one of them will count, and unless you somehow get a promotion to manager, flipping burgers is going to be a tough way to make rent."

"So, I'll find a roommate."

"You better start asking around now and make plans. Start applying for apartments. You can't expect something to magically be open when you wait until the last minute."

Sianna slammed a hand down on the table, tears brimming in her eyes. "Why do you have to be like this? It's Christmas. He's trying to be nice to you even though you've been nothing but mean for weeks."

Momma shot to her feet, glaring at Sianna and then Sam. "Mean? I'm being honest. You need to grow up fast, Sam. Christmas is for children and you're not one of those anymore. I'm going to spend the day with Alberdeen. Her family couldn't visit this year and she's alone."

Sianna's voice rose. "You're leaving?"

"I'm certainly not inviting her here. We can't even have a civil breakfast."

Floored, Sam could only laugh. "And that's our fault? Are you serious?"

"Momma," Sianna scolded. "How can you say that?"

"You'll see. Both of you. You've got it too easy

now. You *both* need to grow up." She stormed over to the stairs.

"Did Dad need to grow up too? I'm starting to see why he left," Sam yelled toward the stairs as she walked down.

Sianna's mouth dropped open.

Already feeling guilty for his outburst without further rebuke from Sianna, Sam grabbed his coat and slammed the front door on his way out to let Momma know he was leaving.

Clearly, that's what she wanted. Him gone.

The warm and tasty breakfast gone cold and sour in his stomach, Sam took off on his bike.

So much for Christmas.

18

Wintery air bit into Sam's face as he raced through the neighborhood. Traffic was light, being Christmas morning. Everyone else was home with their families. Apparently, he didn't have much of one of those anymore.

Adrenaline pumped through his body. Now, more than ever he wished he knew where his father was. No doubt Aralim knew, but it wasn't like the angel would tell him. Aralim only wanted one thing.

Sam rode faster, weaving from sidewalk to street for the hell of it since hardly anyone was on the roads. He rode until his breath came in gasps and he couldn't feel his face. Examining his surroundings, Sam realized he didn't know where he was. He was pretty sure he'd circled around the neighborhood a couple times before heading off toward work, because that was where autopilot had directed him, but after that, one street had led to another.

An open convenience store stood on one corner. A church, a bank, and a carwash rounded out his other options, but all of those appeared to be closed. The street name didn't sound familiar. A smart phone would have been really handy about then, but he'd spent his extra money on Sianna's phone and had, in fact, put the rest aside for when he had to move out. Momma could keep her flipping Amy's Upscale Resale vase that he'd gone to three resale shops, two of them twice, to find. Those places didn't take returns anyway.

He parked his bike in the rack outside the convenience store, and went inside. He hadn't grabbed his wallet when he'd left, but at least he could get warm.

It only took a few minutes for the cold to wear off before his overworked muscles informed him that he was plenty warm inside. He started to sweat. The clerk watched him warily. Sam realized he was the only other person in the store.

Knowing he wasn't going to buy anything and not wanting to chance getting accused of shoplifting, because that would just make Momma's day, he left.

Back on his bike, he pedaled slowly down the street back the way he'd come, looking for anything familiar. It took two blocks for him to figure out where he was and half an hour to work his way toward school. No one would be there either, but there were benches there, some tucked out of the chilly wind. At least it wasn't snowing and the roads were clear. The sun was even shining, not that any of that made him feel cheery. If anything, it made him angrier. How dare the world be a happy, sunny place while he was miserable?

He passed people loading gift bags into their cars, hugging family as they parted ways. The smell of a turkey in a deep fryer in some guy's driveway caught his nose. Sam thought of the little ham in the refrigerator at home that he'd been going to put in the oven and the pie and pasta salad that he'd worked on the night before.

His legs slowed. He could go home and apologize. Or if Momma was gone, he could still salvage the day with Sianna. Maybe. He considered the astounded look Sianna had given him when he'd mentioned their father leaving. Salvaging was probably not an option with her either.

When Sam reached the campus, he headed for the side of the sprawling building where there were benches beneath the trees. In the warmer months, people often ate lunch there or hung out after school. The performance hall on the other side of the trees helped enclose the space, blocking some of the wind. He parked his bike and sat down on the cold, metal bench.

Where could he go for the rest of the day? What friends he might have hung out with were busy with family. Work was closed. He didn't have his wallet to go anywhere that was open. He shoved his hands in his pockets to get warm. One hand wrapped around a plastic bag: the pills Mike had given him.

Sam studied the bag in his hand, the four innocent pills offering an escape from everything. He took one from the bag.

Why the hell not. Merry Christmas.

He swallowed it and leaned back, getting comfortable and trying to ignore the cold. He watched the bare trees blow in the wind for a while until everything started to feel a little better.

When Sam finally went home, he didn't look to see if Momma was there. He didn't check in on Sianna. He went to the fridge, got the pie he'd baked, noted two pieces were missing, and took it, along with a fork to his room.

He sat on his bed. Movement out of his window caught his attention. Henry, with Mrs. Harris by his side and a helmet on his head, was taking a wobbly ride on a shiny new red bike in their driveway. The boy grinned from ear to ear, laughing and chatting away with his mother. She smiled and laughed with him, clapping when he made it back up the drive by himself.

Sam sat on his bed, ate his pie, and spent the rest of the evening hating everyone in varying degrees.

When he woke the next morning, other than using the bathroom, he didn't leave his room. He opened his laptop and contemplated getting some work done, but words blurred into meaningless lines on the screen. He ate the last of the pie and then still had five hours to kill before he had to go to work. Remembering the weightless feeling from the pill he'd taken, he reached around until he found where he'd dropped his coat and pulled one of the remaining pills from the pocket. Home and warm in his room, he was safe. It wasn't like he was out doing anything stupid. All he wanted was a little relief, a brief vacation from the obligations of his looming future. The pill wasn't as good as what Aralim had shown him, but it was better than nothing. Sam was very fed up with all the nothing. He'd tried. He'd tried very hard. But none of that mattered.

Sam swallowed the pill.

Knocking on his door roused Sam from his absent-minded watching of Henry doing loops on his new bike in the driveway next door.

"What?" he snapped, not bothering to get up.

The knob rattled. "Samuel, open this door."

Groaning, he worked himself off the bed and unlocked the door. He opened it just enough to look down on his mother.

"I left that vase on the table. You make sure that goes back today."

"No returns. Keep it."

She scowled. "I'm heading to work. Be sure to check on your sister before you go."

"Sure, whatever." He shut his door, not wanting to deal with the negativity.

"You better be sure to get your school work done," she shouted through his door.

He didn't bother to reply, turning back to view out the window.

Henry tipped over on his bike. Mrs. Harris leapt out of her seat on the porch and ran over to scoop him up, checking every inch of him over. When she set him back on his feet, Henry was smiling again. He ran back to his bike and continued his loops like nothing had happened.

Watching was starting to make him sad and maybe angry. He couldn't decide which, but he didn't like it. He set an alarm for work and fell back on his pillow. Closing his eyes, he pretended what he was feeling was the soft feathers of Aralim's wings surrounding him. That everything was alright. That for a little while, he didn't have a care in the world.

19

It had taken two weeks of not turning in a single assignment for the school to do anything about it. But really, why bother? If he fulfilled the task Aralim had assigned him, he was going to jail. No one in there cared one bit if he had a diploma. And Momma had made it clear she was kicking him out regardless. So why not take it easy for what little time he had left? In the two months after the holiday break, he'd given up all pretense of putting money away for moving out. Mike got most of it in exchange for the pills that made life tolerable. Not that they would cover up much tonight. He'd gotten the email from school before he'd left, sighting his lack of effort and that he was now failing all his classes. Not even a miracle from Aralim could pull off his graduation. But it was all Aralim's fault anyway so screw it.

When Mike pulled in the driveway to drop him off after work. Sam didn't wait for the storm surely waiting inside. If he'd gotten an email, Momma had gotten a phone call or an email or both. He popped an extra pill for tolerance, thanked Mike for the ride, and went inside.

Momma stood with her arm's crossed right inside the front door. "What on earth do you think you're doing?"

"Coming home from work?" he said, knowing full well that wasn't what she meant but not caring.

"Samuel, school called. It was that harping principal lady again. You know I hate talking to her." Momma shook her head, glaring at him. "You're failing. Everything. Again. What the hell is wrong with you?"

As if summoned by the yelling, Sianna crept out of her room. Dressed in sweats and a baggy t-shirt, her standard outfit the past couple of months, she edged toward the kitchen. Sam could hear her rummaging through the cupboards.

"What are you doing in there, girl? You just ate an hour ago. You're emptying the fridge faster than I can fill it," Momma yelled toward the kitchen. "You're going to want to fit into all your cute clothes at some point, Sianna. You can't wear sweats forever."

Sam grimaced. "Leave Sianna alone."

"One kid failing and another packing on the pounds," Momma grumbled. "Puts me in the running for Mother of the Year."

Even with the pills taking the edge off, anger bubbled to the forefront. "Not everything is about you."

Her eyes went wide and her head cocked in that angle that let him know he'd hit a nerve. "What did you say?"

"Nothing," Sam snapped. He started for his room.

"I wasn't done talking to you."

"I'm done."

"Samuel!"

He kept walking.

"If you go into that room before I'm finished, you better start packing."

With each step, Sam considered who he could stay with and what he needed to pack. It wasn't like he was going to be free all that long.

Sianna stormed into the living room, facing off with Momma. Sam halted his escape and turned around.

"You can't make him leave," Sianna decreed. "We need him to help pay the bills."

While Sam didn't fully appreciate only being needed for financial reasons, he was grateful for the sisterly mediation.

"We'll get by," Momma said firmly.

"No, Momma, we won't." Sianna looked over Momma's shoulder to Sam and grimaced as she shook her head. "I'm pregnant. I need both of you.

I need you to help. I need you to get along." Tears welled in her eyes. "I can't do this by myself."

He'd known Sianna would have to tell Momma at some point, she couldn't hide behind the sweats and baggy shirts much longer. That she'd divulged the truth so that he might be able to stay, almost made him cry too. He darted around Momma, who hadn't moved or said a word, to hug his sister.

"You're not by yourself. Whether I'm here or not, alright?" he said.

Sianna sniffed and nodded against his shoulder.

"No," Momma said quietly. "How could you?" She shook her head. "Sianna, how could you ruin your life like this?"

Sam wanted to scream at her, to tell her that it wasn't Sianna's fault, but that wasn't his truth to tell. Instead, he squeezed his sister tightly, offering what support he could.

Sianna released Sam and glared at Momma. "Just like we ruined your life? Is that what you're saying?"

"No. You're too young. You've got your whole future ahead of you."

"Just like you did when you got pregnant with Sam? Yeah, that's exactly what you're saying."

Momma groaned. "You don't have to keep it. You could put it up for adoption. You could get your life back, go to college, find a nice boy in a few years and start a family when you're ready. When you can afford it. When you actually want a baby."

Sianna thrust her fists onto her hips. "Is that what your momma told you? Well, you know what? I didn't plan on this but this baby is mine and I'm keeping it." She turned on her heel, strode into her room, and slammed the door.

"That's not..." his mother said, looking straight at Sam. "I didn't..."

"Sure." A disgusted noise escaped Sam's lips before he clamped them shut. He started for his room.

"Sam!" she called after him.

As much as he wanted to spin around and yell in her face, he merely stopped in place and half turned his head to watch her out of the corner of his eye over his shoulder.

"We'll talk about your future plans later? I need some time to think."

She couldn't just give him a reprieve? Couldn't offer further reassurance that he hadn't, in fact, ruined her life by coming into it? Sam kept his response to a slight nod and continued into his room. He closed the door and sank down into the bed.

Maybe Aralim was right, putting off his task was just making life more difficult for everyone. If he'd killed Henry right away, he wouldn't have gotten so attached to the kid. He could have gone off to jail thinking Momma still loved him. Sianna might have free-willed herself into a better situation in which to get pregnant. Sam fell back into the bed and sighed.

Delaying wasn't helping anyone.

Though he was resolved to the task Aralim had assigned him and he'd gotten into the closet twice, Sam hadn't worked up the nerve to take the gun out of its hiding place. Once he got it that far, he knew that completing his task wouldn't be long after.

It had been three weeks since Sianna had announced that she was pregnant. Three very long, awkwardly quiet weeks. Momma had picked up extra shifts at work. While that meant he hadn't had to talk much to his mother, she also hadn't talked much to Sianna.

"I think she hates me," Sianna said, staring glumly into the half-eaten bowl of cereal she was having for dinner.

"I doubt she'd be working extra shifts to put a little money away if that were the case."

"She never apologized."

"She probably won't." Not after Momma's first reaction full of adoption and ruining lives. First reactions were the truthful ones. She'd had plenty of time to make up for what she'd said, but had made no effort to do so.

Sianna abandoned her spoon in the bowl. "Do you think if I tell her the truth of what happened, she'll be more on my side? Like she used to be?"

Sam pondered his sister, her cheeks a little rounder. She rubbed circles over her stomach as she sat back, smoothing the fabric over her rounding belly that was otherwise masked by the over-sized shirt.

"No. She'll push even harder for you to give up the baby." He sighed. "It wouldn't surprise me if she hunted Rolando down and tried to press charges against him herself. At the very least, she'd end up in a screaming match with his parents on their lawn."

Sianna grimaced. "It wasn't like that. Not exactly. With Rolando, I mean. He didn't force..." She rubbed her face and stared at the bowl, her cheeks flushed. "I didn't mean it to go that far. It just sort of happened and when I got mad that it had, he got mad too. Like really mad."

"So mad that the side of the road in the middle of the night was a better place to be?"

Sianna nodded.

He was relieved to know that what he'd thought had happened, wasn't entirely true. Not that it changed anything.

"Momma is on your side, Sianna. Just not

exactly in the way you want her to be."

And after he worked up the nerve to get the gun, Momma would be all Sianna had. Sam's stomach churned.

"Give her some time to get used to the idea. You've had months to come to terms with it. She's only had a few weeks. It's not like she's going to toss you out."

Sianna's hand curled into a fist beside her bowl. "She's not still harping on you to move out, is she?"

With his future looming, Sam steeled himself to giving Sianna fair warning. What was going to happen would put a strain on her and Momma too. A strain neither of them needed on top of the baby. He'd do what little he could to prepare her.

"She's barely said a word to me, but I'll be leaving anyway. She'll be better with you once I'm gone. More on your side."

Desperation lit in her eyes. "Sam, you can't leave."

He stood and took his bowl to the sink so he didn't have to face her.

"Trust me, she'll be much more supportive when you're all she has left."

"You said you'd be here. That you'd be with me," Sianna pleaded.

Aralim's contract terms played through Sam's mind. "I will, I promise. But like Momma, just not quite in the way that you want."

Sianna's chair screeched over the floor as she pushed herself to her feet. "If you leave, I'll never forgive you," she yelled before storming off to her room. She slammed the door.

Though his hands shook and his heart was heavy, Sam was glad. As long as Sianna was in her room, he couldn't get to the gun.

20

February brought a break in the continual grey skies of winter. Sunlight sparkled on the dusting of snow outside Sam's bedroom window. A beam shot in around the edge of the blanket to highlight the shoe box containing the gun and bullets that sat on the floor against the far wall. Sam sat on the edge of his bed, his skin crawling, feeling Aralim close even if the angel couldn't be seen. It wasn't like the sunlight was being subtle.

Use the gun, Sam. Complete your task, Sam. Do it.

Sam pressed his hands to his head and squeezed, desperately wanting the voice to stop. He couldn't even tell if it was his or Aralim's anymore. The pills made the voice quieter, but he was out. He wouldn't see Mike until tomorrow and drowning the voice was becoming increasingly more expensive. If he was going to save any money for Sianna and the baby, he needed to act soon.

"Sam," Momma shouted. "Get out here now!"

Gritting his teeth in preparation for whatever she was going to yell at him about, Sam again wished he had a pill or two left as he opened his bedroom door.

At least she hadn't been harping on him to pack his stuff and move out yet, but maybe she was about to. Not that it mattered, he was generally packed already. He figured it would make it easier on both of them when the police took him away, less to clean up when he was out of their lives.

"What?" he snapped.

"Something's wrong with the baby. With Sianna. Go sit with her while I call the doctor." She pointed toward the living room.

He nodded, his annoyance forgotten in a rush of concern. Sam hurried to the couch where Sianna sat, hunched over and pale. He sat down beside her.

"What's wrong?"

Sianna shook her head. "I don't know. It hurts. I'm bleeding," she whispered.

Sam's first thought was to run back to his room and do anything he could to summon Aralim. How was he supposed to be reborn as Sianna's baby if there was no baby?

Sianna grabbed his hand before he could move. "Don't leave."

"I'm right here."

She nodded, breathing in loudly through her nose and out through her mouth. "I'm scared," she whispered.

"Me too." And not only for her baby, but for his sister. For his own fate.

He desperately wanted to get to his room, to yell at the angel, to demand that it fix whatever was wrong, but he didn't dare leave Sianna's side. Not to mention her iron grip on his hand wasn't letting him go anywhere.

Off in the kitchen, he made out his mother talking on the phone. She sounded just as worried as he felt.

"We'll figure this out," he assured Sianna.

She nodded but didn't look convinced.

Momma darted into the living room. "I'm taking you to the emergency room. Sam, help me get her into the car."

Sam stood and gently pulled Sianna to her feet. With one arm around her, he guided her to the front closet where Momma got her into a coat and then they both took a side and led her out to the car. Sam helped her slide into the passenger seat and then opened the rear door.

"Stay here," Momma ordered. "They're going to do an exam and whatever else. Woman's business. You'd just be sitting in the waiting room the whole time. I'll call home when I know anything."

"You're sure?" he asked Sianna more than his mother.

Sianna glanced at Momma and then back to Sam. She nodded, lips pinched tight and worry creasing her forehead.

"Alright. I'll be waiting for your call."

He watched them pull out of the driveway and disappear down the street. His heart wanted to go with them but his head guided his feet back inside so he could take out his anger on a deserving target.

"Aralim!" he yelled the moment he entered the empty house.

A blazing light blinded Sam, making him stagger and bang his shin on the table beside the couch.

The angel had the gall to glare at him. Gleaming feathered wings arched out behind it, flexing like it might take off at any second.

"Delays will cost you," Aralim's voice rang out, echoing, expanding and contracting.

"Cost me?" Anger sped through Sam's veins, pounding in his ears. He rushed at the angel, jabbing his finger into the shimmering and very solid chest. "If you hurt my sister—"

Pain shot through his finger as if he'd set fire to his skin. Sam pulled his hand back, cradling it against his chest.

"The only one hurting your sister, is you."

"Me? I haven't done anything to her. I'm doing everything I can to help her. Her and her baby."

Aralim's thin brows rose. The angel shook its head slowly. "A baby without a soul can only survive so long, even in the womb."

"Without a soul?"

Aralim waved his hand in Sam's direction. "Yours is still in this body."

Beneath his hand, Sam's heart thundered in his chest. He could wait no longer. Sianna needed him.

If only he had a couple of pills to soften the edges of what he had to do, anything to make it hurt less.

Aralim merely watched him, saying nothing, wings moving in slow motion, up and down as if they were breathing on their own.

Sam drew a shuddering breath and forced one foot to follow the other until he reached his room. Heaven was waiting.

It was everything before he got there that made him take a quick detour to the bathroom to purge the contents of his stomach into the toilet. When he was done, he wiped a wet cloth over his face with a trembling hand and emerged to find Aralim gone.

Knowing what he had to do, Sam forced himself over to the box on the floor. He opened it, pulled out the gun, running his fingers over the cold, smooth barrel. Just like he'd seen on the video he'd found on the internet, he opened the box of ammunition and loaded the gun.

As he watched his fingers loading the gun, holding it, a distance formed between his mind and his body, almost as if he'd stepped outside of himself. He was somewhere else, safe while he watched someone else hold the loaded gun. Someone else's eye sighted the faded drawing of a horse he'd done years ago in art class while a finger rested on the trigger. Someone else resolved himself to the knowledge that he would shoot the gun today.

That he would kill today.

The horse drawing blurred. Hot tears ran down Sam's cheeks.

He stood there, locked in place as time passed in a distant blur, cursing Aralim, God, and whoever's freewill act had made it necessary for Henry's soul to be needed elsewhere.

Not only would he ruin his own mother's life with this act, but Mrs. Harris's too.

The phone rang.

With the gun in one hand, Sam hurried to the kitchen to answer the call.

Momma's voice sounded wrong, too quiet, scared. "The baby is barely moving. Sam, I know I said some terrible things, but I wouldn't wish losing a baby on anyone, especially not Sianna."

"I know." What else was there to say?

"They're going to try some things, keep her overnight for observation. I'm going to stay here with her as long as they'll let me. Pray for your sister and this baby. They need all the help they can get."

"I will." He waited for her to hang up. This was more than she'd spoken to him in weeks.

"Sam?"

He tried to subdue the edge he'd found himself using in every conversation with her lately. "What?"

"I've been hard on you, but I want you to know that I do love you. You know that right?"

His throat threatened to close up. Sam wiped his wet cheeks with his sleeve.

"Yeah, Momma, I know. Love you too. Take care of Sianna."

"I will."

The phone clicked. Sam held the cold plastic a moment longer, playing his mother's voice over in his head, knowing he'd never hear her say that again. Even if he did get to talk to her in the future, it would be all ranting and wailing. There would be no more soft words between them.

With the phone returned to the cradle, he went to Sianna's room, opening the door to take in all that was his sister. Soon baby things would take the place of her tumble of clothing on the floor. He imagined a crib next to her bed, Sianna singing soft lullabies.

Sam closed the door and stood in the living room. Sunlight sparkling on glass caught his eye. Momma had finally put the Christmas vase on the table where her mother's vase had been. He smiled, imagining her walking through the room with a fussy grandbaby on her shoulder.

The weight of the gun in his hand urged Sam back to his room where he pulled the blanket from the window. Henry peddled his bike in a circle on his driveway. Mrs. Harris must have been inside, probably with a window open or sitting close to one. She rarely let Henry out of her sight.

He took in the smiling boy, his cheeks pink in the chill air as his little legs pumped up and down. He wore a red coat, zipped up. Snowflakes drifted down lazily, but the sun shone brightly, making the air just warm enough to keep the plowed-clean driveway free of more snow.

Not trusting that his lack of skill and shaking hands would make him an accurate shot by any means, Sam considered a logical reason to get close to Henry. Closer would mean less chance of missing. God, Aralim and anyone else up high knew he didn't want to have to fire twice. Pulling the trigger once was going to be hard enough.

Tears again welled in his eyes, blurring his vision as he reached for Henry's Squidman. He shoved it in his pocket and sniffed. This was for Sianna. For Momma too, because she'd be heartbroken if anything happened to Sianna, and maybe even the baby that she'd been so adamantly against. Not for Aralim or any stupid agreement he'd signed.

Drawing a ragged breath, Sam took one last look at his room and its paltry contents, most of which were in boxes or neat stacks on the floor. None of it mattered.

He walked to the front door with slow dragging steps, his feet knowing where they had to go, but resisting as much as they were able. Peering out the window beside the door, he was relieved to see that the neighbors all seemed to be inside. The last thing he needed was an audience.

Not trusting that he'd have the nerve to draw the gun again if it left his hand, he didn't dare tuck it anywhere. Instead, he held it to his side, pressing it against his pants. With his heart thundering in his chest, Sam opened the door.

21

S am!" Henry squealed, racing toward him. "Look what I can do!"

Sam forced what he hoped looked like a smile as he slowly walked up his driveway and out onto the sidewalk. Even on this deadly mission, walking over Mrs. Harris's immaculately cut lawn felt wrong.

"Watch!" Henry pulled up on the handlebars to lift the front tire half an inch off the concrete. "Pretty cool, huh?"

Sam nodded, stepping off the sidewalk onto Mrs. Harris's driveway. The sun might be keeping the snow from building up, but the chilly air made Sam realize he hadn't put on a coat. It wouldn't matter anyway. Surely the police car would be warm. As soon as he fired the gun, someone would call them. People might not be outside, but cars were in enough driveways to indicate that plenty of families were home.

Fumbling in his pocket, Sam pried Henry's Squidman out. He held it up so Henry could plainly see it.

"You wanna play?" Henry asked. He pressed the brakes on his bike and put his feet down to stand.

Sam swallowed hard, walking closer. "Sure," he croaked. What he wanted to say was 'I'm sorry. Run inside. Call the police!' But none of that would help Siana or her baby. It wouldn't fulfill his agreement with Aralim. Delays were only hurting people. Maybe people he didn't even realize. What if there was another pregnant woman somewhere with a baby waiting for Henry's soul? Was she scared and hurting too?

Henry cocked his head, watching Sam. His eyebrows lowered, and concern lined his childish face. "Sam?"

"It will all be okay, little man," Sam managed to say as he lifted the gun.

Henry froze. "Sam?" he whispered.

A curtain parted in the front window. Mrs. Harris's face peeked out. The curtain dropped.

Pulse hammering in his ears, Sam knew he only had seconds before she ran outside. Before she begged him to drop the gun. Could he shoot Henry in front his mother? Bile rose in this throat.

Sam took aim and rested his sweaty finger on the trigger. "I'm sorry."

Aiming at Henry was far different than aiming at the drawing of the horse. But he had to. Sam's hand shook. He took a deep breath. Sweat poured out of his body as his finger squeezed.

He fired.

The front door banged open. Footsteps thundered across the porch.

Henry's gaze locked with Sam's. A small hole marked the front of his coat. Henry's fingers slipped from the handlebars. He crumpled to the driveway. The bike fell with him. Blood blossomed on the front of his coat.

His mouth hanging open, Henry panted. Sunlight glinted off the slowly spinning spokes, momentarily blinding Sam. The air, the sun, Henry bleeding on the driveway, it all went distant until all Sam knew was his pulse thundering through his head. Black spots edged his vision.

One thought drove through all the haze. Henry deserved his full attention in these last moments. Sam shook his head. He dropped the gun. The hard plastic of the Squidman action figure bit into his other hand.

Sam remembered how Aralim had restored the apples with a simple touch. He could bring Henry back. He could undo this, erase the horror flooding Sam with every passing second.

"Aralim! Please save him!"

Maybe this was all some sort of test, like one

of those stories from the bible. Surely this little kid didn't have to actually die. He would be saved. Everything would go back to normal now that Sam had proven his faith.

But the angel didn't appear, and Henry didn't cry. He just stopped moving. Like he'd frozen there.

Henry was gone.

Sam let out a sob.

Surely something would indicate that he'd fulfilled his task? Shouldn't he feel relieved? But he didn't. There was only an immense self-loathing and a terrible weight on his shoulders, like he was holding up the entire sky all by himself.

He tried to look anywhere else, but he couldn't tear himself away from Henry's body. Sirens, he'd hear them any minute. The police would take him away. He wouldn't have to look at what he'd done as soon as they arrived. They'd have him face down on the concrete for sure.

Mrs. Harris screamed. A shot rang out.

Sam stared at the gun he'd dropped. It wasn't him. He couldn't hurt anyone else. He wouldn't. His job was done.

Pain ripped into his shoulder, breaking his trance. He looked to find Mrs. Harris holding a gun with both hands, standing just like the police officers did on TV. She was pale and crying.

He glanced at his shoulder. Blood soaked through his shirt. Was this what Henry had felt?

She let out a horrible wail that made Sam tremble even more than getting shot. Tears ran down his cheeks. He'd known she would be devastated. But knowing and hearing, seeing, it was all so much worse than he'd imagined. A little voice in his head told him he should run, that he should at least get down on the ground. But he deserved this, didn't he?

Aralim wasn't a guardian angel either. If it hadn't shown up to save Henry, it certainly wouldn't save him.

She fired again. This time the impact tore into his stomach.

Sam's legs went out from under him, landing him on the concrete driveway. His head hit so hard that his vision blinked out for a moment. When it cleared, he stared up at the white puffy clouds drifting overhead. Had Henry seen them too?

He turned his head so he could see Henry. Maybe if he could do just one last thing, Mrs. Harris would understand that he hadn't wanted to hurt her son. That he hadn't meant to hurt her, or that he'd forgotten the nice things she'd done for him. Sam turned on his side so he could get his arms under himself. Still gripping Squidman in one hand, he started to pull himself closer.

Sirens. There they finally were, whining in the distance. The police would be here soon to help Mrs. Harris take care of Henry.

If they gave him a few more moments, he could return Squidman to the boy who'd loved him. He could make this better.

Sam pulled himself closer. His empty hand landed on the gun he'd dropped. He grabbed it to fling the horrible thing away, to put it as far from Henry as possible.

"How could you!" Mrs. Harris screamed at him from where she now stood over Henry, her gun still in her hands.

The sirens grew louder.

Sam's arms gave out. With his father's gun in one hand and Squidman in the other, he dropped back to the ground. Mrs. Harris fired again.

His breath caught. He wasn't even sure where the third bullet had hit. It didn't matter. The distance and black spots closed in on him again.

The sirens grew unbearably loud. A car pulled into the end of the driveway. Doors clicked open and feet raced toward him.

"Drop the gun!" A man bellowed.

Sam couldn't. His fingers weren't listening anymore. He couldn't feel his feet either. Or maybe was all of his arms and legs. Maybe it was everything.

Another car arrived, screeching to a halt. People raced around him. A yanking sensation along with a clunking metal sound followed by a scraping noise made him guess that someone kicked the gun away. All the bodies were shadows and everything seemed distant except sounds. Someone was talking to Mrs. Harris. She was sobbing. The only word he could make out was "Henry."

That was the one word that mattered. Not a word, he reminded himself. A person.

A blinding light cut through the shadows around Sam. Vast white wings blocked out the sirens, the rushing bodies, and even Mrs. Harris's sobbing.

Aralim smiled down on him. "You matter too, Sam."

Sam shook his head, or he wanted to. His body wasn't cooperating anymore. *"I don't,"* he thought at the angel.

"Everyone matters." Aralim stroked Sam's cheek. "The boy wasn't the only one who was needed elsewhere."

Sam's heart stuttered. He tried to take another breath but found he couldn't. He didn't have to. His lungs didn't ask for more.

"Why didn't you tell me?"

The angel smiled sadly. "I did. You were so focused on the task that you didn't stop to hear all that I was saying."

"All you said was that my soul would go to Sianna's baby."

Aralim nodded. "The rest was you thinking

you knew the plan for your future. You envisioned the worst because that's what you thought you deserved."

"*Oh,*" Sam whispered in his thoughts.

"You've repaired this section of humanity's weave, Sam." Aralim helped him to his feet, pulling Sam gently from the body that he no longer required. "Let's get you where you need to be so you can do far more than what you've done here."

Sam pondered the sensation of soft feathers against the body he could feel but couldn't see. The wings blocked out the sight of the bloody shell he'd inhabited. Aralim held Sam's hands but his feet didn't register anything beneath him, lending to the sensation of floating.

"*I won't remember? Any of this? Not Momma or Sianna? Not even Henry?*"

"Not exactly, no. Would you want to?"

There were parts of his life he did desperately want to keep. Feeling safe in Momma's arms, Sianna's sparkling laugh that made him smile just thinking about it, the fuzzy memories of working with his father in the garage when he was little, kind words from teachers and his boss, the smell of Pastor Joe's aftershave that always meant they'd have a few good meals. He vividly remembered how bittersweet it had felt when a little boy had pressed his prized possession into Sam's hand.

Tears welled in eyes Sam no longer had. "*No.*

I don't want to remember."

Aralim hugged him, pulling Sam against the angel's skin that had burned him when he'd touched it in anger. Now there was only comfort. A heavy sense of peace washed through him, pushing all his thoughts, every regret, and very last, the memories he'd clung to, out of his mind.

Time lost all meaning. He stayed there with Aralim, comfortable and at peace, wrapped in the wings of the angel.

"There now, you have somewhere to be." Aralim kissed his forehead and then released his hold on Sam.

The angel turned him around and gave him a gentle push.

The whiteness parted in front of Sam. Unsure, he turned back, but Aralim was gone. Everything went black and he was terrified, alone, unknowing, lost.

And then the white light was back, but it was different now, not as brilliant. The air was cold. The shapes around him were giant, sounds booming. Something grabbed him, and he couldn't do a thing about it other than scream, begging for whatever this was to end so he could go back to the soft peaceful place he'd been.

22

Sianna peered through the window at the children playing in the next room. She leaned forward in her chair to pull her vibrating phone from her purse on the floor. Checking who was calling, she sighed as she answered.

"Yes, Momma, we're both fine. The center is taking very good care of us. We'll be home in a few days just like I told you when you called last time."

"I worry about you," Momma said.

Reminding herself that her mother was home alone and had been for a week now, she softened her tone. "I worry about you too. Are you feeling alright?"

"I'm fine."

Though the doctors had said Momma was clear of cancer thanks to catching it early, Sianna still kept a close eye on her. She would be forever thankful for the program's excellent and affordable medical care.

"The stupid, hairy cat misses Sammy."

Sianna laughed, managing to stifle most of it so she didn't disturb the other parents in the observation room. The cat could never replace her brother, but Sianna needed someone she could confide in, especially with having to live with her moody mother and a rambunctious four-year-old in a two-bedroom apartment. Mr. Fluffles never betrayed her confidence, and he was Sammy's best friend when they were between screening sessions at the center.

"It's too quiet here when you're both gone," her mother said softly.

"I know, Momma. Three more days. Give Alberdeen a call. I'm sure she'll come over to keep you company."

"Yeah, maybe I'll do that."

Sianna had a feeling she wouldn't. Momma talked to her best friend on the phone once a week, but she rarely left the apartment unless it was to go somewhere with Sianna and Sammy. She was sure people were still talking about the shooting four years ago in their old neighborhood. The day her brother had shot the neighbor's little boy. Her and Momma had known Sam was going through a bad time. She'd even suspected he'd been on drugs, but she'd never thought he was as bad off as he apparently had been.

Her big brother had threatened to kill Sammy's

father. He'd been on drugs. The police had busted the kid who gave him rides to work for being a dealer. They'd painted Sam into a stereotype in no time flat. High school drop-out druggie from a broken home with a bad temper. The gun had been registered to their father, but Sianna had no idea where Sam had found it or if it had been before or after the police had searched their house. She didn't want to think that's who he was. It wasn't who he was to her. He'd been her brother, her best friend, and she'd had no regrets about naming her son after Sam no matter what anyone else thought about the statistic they'd turned him into.

"Do you still have meals in the fridge, Momma?"

"More than I could eat even if Alberdeen did come over. You always make too much food, girl."

"I just want to make sure you're taken care of."

"The pie was very good. Just like the one—" Her voice wavered.

"I know, Momma. I know." Every time they had one of their ten-day screening sessions, Sianna made a pie for Momma using the recipe she'd found in Sam's room when she'd cleaned it out before they'd moved. Having a piece with Momma before she and Sammy left had become their ritual.

Sianna spotted one of the other mothers making her way over, two cookies in one hand and two coffees in the other.

"I gotta go, Momma. We'll see you soon. Love

you."

"Love you too."

Sianna ended the call and slid the phone back into her purse. The screen might have been scratched and the features were outdated, but it still worked and she wasn't getting rid of Sam's last Christmas gift until she had to.

"Everything alright?" Natasha asked, handing her one of the coffees and a cookie.

"Yes, thanks. Lonely mother."

Natasha settled into the chair next to Sianna. "Scott isn't wild about these long sessions either, but one of us has to stay home with the other kids and the dog. He came here once, but after seeing it was all pretty benign, he decided he'd rather stay home and let me have a little time off from the chaos."

"That's nice of him." Sianna sighed inwardly, knowing Natasha's next question. They'd been friends here for four years, and Mr. Fluffles didn't offer advice like humans did. Sometimes she did need to talk to a human.

"How are things with Rolando?"

"Good. I think? We don't talk much other than about Sammy but he's taking him camping for the weekend on his next visitation. He'll be home from college for spring break."

Natasha smiled. "That's good. I know those first couple of years were hard on your own. Well, other than your mother, but that's a different kind of hard, isn't it?" She chuckled. "But isn't having Sammy's father involved, at least a little bit, better?"

"It is." She'd totally balked at the idea when Natasha had suggested contacting Rolando, but she was glad she eventually had. Knowing how much she and Sam had missed their absent father, and wondering if having him around, even if only to some degree, would have changed things for Sam, she wanted to do things differently for her son.

"Henri misses Sammy between sessions. As much as I hate being away from the girls for so long, it's good to see those two having such a good time together."

Sianna nodded, watching the two boys gleefully battling with a pile of action figures. She sipped her coffee and nibbled at her cookie. She never would have imagined that one nurse seeing she needed help and slipping her a business card as she'd left the hospital with one-day old Sammy would have changed their lives to such a degree. But here they were. She'd called the number on the card and that had led to a paid baby formula trial. The trial had led to them being selected for this study in accelerated learning that now paid for her apartment, food, and travel to and from study sessions. She'd never known that nurse's name, but not a day went by that she wasn't thankful for that one small act of kindness.

"Between sessions, Sammy incessantly asks how long it will be before he sees Henri again. I think even Mr. Fluffles gets sick of the question after a while."

Natasha laughed behind her hand as she finished off her cookie. She washed it down with a gulp of coffee. "I wanted to ask if you've given any more thought to enrollment for next year? Scott is on the fence, but if Sammy signs up that's all the sway I'll need."

Sianna had purposefully left the forms at home. Sammy might only be four but she wanted to talk to him about the option before she jumped on the opportunity. An entirely free accelerated learning program through college level that he could complete in ten years? He'd get the education she and Sam had only dreamed about, the one Momma had wanted for both of them.

In the room on the other side of the window, the instruction team called for the children's attention. Twelve four-year-olds dutifully put down their toys and returned to the three rows of tables to resume their studies.

"Can you imagine what these kids could accomplish together when they get older?" Sianna asked.

"If they all continue?" Natasha asked with a teasing grin.

Seeing the kids all together and how eager to learn they were, knowing how far ahead they already were from typical preschoolers, she wanted him to take the opportunity. But it would be his choice. She wouldn't take that away from him.

Sianna nodded. "Yes, assuming they all continue."

Natasha beamed a radiant smile at the children beyond the window. "They could change the world."

About the Author

Jean Davis lives in West Michigan with her musical husband, two attention-craving terriers and a small flock of chickens and ducks. When not ruining fictional lives from the comfort of her writing chair, she can be found devouring books and sushi, weeding her flower garden, or picking up hundreds of sticks while attempting to avoid the abundant snake population that also shares her yard. She writes an array of speculative fiction.

Find links to all of her books, updates on new projects, and sign up for her mailing list at www.jeandavisauthor.com. You'll also find her on Facebook and Instagram at JeanDavisAuthor, and on Goodreads and Amazon.